SIMON WARD

Finding Love in 2045

Second edition

ISBN: 9798623795137

This book was professionally typeset on Reedsy.
Find out more at reedsy.com

Acknowledgement

Many thanks for beta reading suggestions from Jason Pinaster, Bill Williams, Jean Jenkins, Jess James and Amy Smith. All errors remain mine.

The technology details are either complete fiction or developmental work referred to in the publication Exponential Investor which discusses new technologies.

Author Pages:
   https://simonwardauthor.wordpress.com
   or twitter @s111ssw

Finding Love in 2045 is a future set, adult romantic drama.

Mia, 25, strives to find a guy who will follow the traditional rules of courtship, but she's in the wrong era. Stuck in 2045, she's more vulnerable than ever as her craving for a deeper connection grows.

The popularity of AI sexbots provide a further challenge to find someone not intent on instant gratification.

Mia thinks she's found her man but is once again left deflated. Family issues also come to a head and dump her at rock bottom.

Who can lift her out of her malaise and bring her the love she desperately seeks?

Mia's transformation into a sexually confident woman begins, but she'll face more setbacks before she finds a love that will last a lifetime.

Chapter 1

After messaging back and forth for a week, Mia gave dating another try with a guy called Ben. At 25, Mia should have been used to the dating scene, but she'd been born into an era without chivalry and courtship. After a video call with him, she agreed to a date in the hope her luck with love would change. Ben was a cut above the rest and had agreed to take her for a meal and an Immersion experience.

Ben raised his hand to knock on the family door as the Foster family house droid opened it. "Good Evening, you must be Ben."

Although house droids were not uncommon, Ben stepped back and mumbled, "Yep, I'm Ben. Is Mia ready?"

"Hi Ben." Mia danced down the stairs nearly tripping. She gave house droid, Tyler, a quick hug and shouted a quick bye to her mom and dad.

"Look after my Mia," Tyler said, as Ben led her to the waiting autonomous taxi.

Mia was tingling all over as the taxi pulled away. This was definite progress; her date had come to the house. The dating sites of her mom's day were now more like hook ups for a mechanical exchange of juices. The guys Mia had contacted before requested her to come around to their place for sex and dismissed any suggestions to share a meal or watch a movie. Mia had met a few and tried to reason with them about building a genuine connection, but soon got ushered out when she declined to discuss the consent app.

Her closest friend Kat had suggested having sex with them to get into it, but Mia declined, waiting for the right guy. Ben seemed to fit the bill. After a few minutes of quiet, she glanced his way.

"I'm nervous. I really like you," he said.

"Like you too." Mia gave him a coy smile. "I've been looking for a gentleman."

"I shall do my best." Ben returned a more confident smile.

The conversation flowed, and they became more relaxed with each other. Ben impressed Mia when they had their delicious meal. He was the first guy, including her dad, who'd not eaten like it was a race.

They were hand in hand when they entered the Immersion experience. Mia had not been before, and the all-encompassing VR was a plentiful treat, as was holding Ben's hand throughout. His masterful hand reassured her. It set her mind to wondering if her search was over. The theater experience was a romantic comedy, Mia's favorite.   Ben's eyes had the same caring intensity of the leading man with the same short wavy brown hair.

"Great film, did you choose it because you looked like the leading man?" Mia said as they left the theater.

"Maybe?" Ben smiled and squeezed Mia's hand. "Shall we go back to mine?"

Mia's heart raced. She wanted to make an excuse to go home, but her vulnerability took a breather and she figured it was excitement, not panic. She took in a slow breath to calm her pounding heart, "okay."

Ben was also full of nerves. Not including sex droids. It was the first time he was taking a girl back to his place.

Ben mirrored a scene from the movie when the lead had taken his drenched maiden back to his place and made some hot chocolate. Ben and Mia sat on the sofa facing the virtual fireplace as they sipped their drinks and discussed the similarity to their VR experience. The technology had immersed them into each scene, but at Ben's they were experiencing the chocolate aroma and the warmth of the fire for real.

Mia for the first time felt like a movie princess with her handsome prince. As they placed their empty mugs down, Ben leaned in and gave her a gentle kiss to her cheek and like the scene in the movie she responded with their warm lips meeting for the first time. Mia's nervousness melted away with an almighty burst of excitement. Each touch of his firm yet tender hands sent tingles to awaken her.

With a confidence she didn't know she had, she responded by unbuttoning his shirt and slipping her hand onto his hairy chest. "Do you think you should turn the fire down? You're boiling hot."

"No need." He helped himself out of his shirt to reveal his manly chest.

Mia stepped forward and placed her hands on his chest and gave him a cheeky smile. "You've got your own rug."

Ben looked to his mobile by their empty mugs and returned his gaze to Mia. "Shall we continue?" he tentatively asked.

Mia picked up her mobile and nodded with a shy smile. They both tapped through the consent app. When they looked back at each other, Mia tingled with nervous anticipation. Her love life was finally taking hold.

With care, he lifted her tee-shirt over her head. They kissed as they embraced and the heat of their skin connected, taking over the warmth from the fire. Ben filled his chest, inhaling her sweet scent, before he slipped his hand to her waist and after a fumble, unzipped her skirt.

Mia helped and slid her skirt over her hips, letting it fall to the cozy sheepskin rug. Further pulses of pleasure surged through Mia, as he traced kisses with more passion down her side as his hands caressed her body and carefully eased her cotton briefs to her ankles. Whilst he removed his trousers, she sat on the rug and when he joined her; they lay together, sharing a long nuzzling embrace. Their actions had been following the scene in the movie, but when the movie cut to the morning, the ongoing scene for Mia changed.

Ben's moves intensified, becoming less comfortable. His careful caresses replaced with pulling and grabbing as he reached behind to undo her bra. After failing with the clasp, he pulled the front of her bra over her breasts, dragging it over her nipples.

"Ow!" Mia grimaced and pushed against him.

He mumbled a half-arsed apology, before he pressed his lips firmly against hers. With consent confirmed, the firm yet tender touches became more and more rough. His knee pushed between her legs as he lay on top of her, and he eased his erection slowly into her.

He replaced the romantic cuddles and became more like a rabid dog. Mia struggled, but his heavy frame pinned her in place as his pace increased. He banged his groin like a jackhammer into hers. Ben seemed to take her uncomfortable moans and yelps as a compliment before he sunk his teeth into her shoulder as he climaxed.

"You were fantastic," he said as he moved off her and dragged his expired, slimy member over her thigh. With a self-congratulatory smugness, he rolled onto his back and put his hands behind his head.

Without a word, Mia grabbed her things and hurried to the bathroom. Whilst cleaning up and getting dressed, she held back the tears. When she emerged, he was still lying by the fire. "I've got to go," she muttered as she shot out of the door before he could get to his feet.

Mia scuttled away from the house and messaged an autonomous taxi as her eyes became full. The reality of sex had been a far cry from the romantic encounters in her books, and it wasn't something she planned to repeat anytime soon.

The following day Ben rang for another date and it mortified him to hear she hadn't enjoyed it and pleaded for another chance. "I thought girls liked it rough."

"You didn't listen. It was love I wanted, not sex." Mia sobbed.

"I already love you. I'll be more gentle next time."

"There won't be a next time!"

Ben continued to plead but her dad overheard the conversation and with Mia upset he took the phone. "Listen Pal, she doesn't want to see you again. Fuck Off!" He ended the call.

Mia ran upstairs and buried her face in a pillow. Tyler followed her, "Are you okay?" he asked as he peeked his head around the door.

Tyler reached a bear off a shelf and passed it to Mia.

She glanced up from the pillow and wiped her eyes. "Thanks Tyler."

"Anything for you. As always." He said with care.

"No more upgrades." She said cuddling the bear.

Tyler smiled as she buried her face back into the pillow. Mia always hated the change when he received an upgrade. Even though he became more lifelike, she would shun him for a few days and tell him to change back. But they'd soon be buddies again.

Ben called a week later, but the protective Tyler blocked his call to avoid further distress to Mia. Meanwhile, Mia's malaise deepened. She deleted the app and spent hours in her room despondent with a loveless life passing her by.

Her only pleasure was from reading romance novels and gazing at her image of James Dean, the 1950s heartthrob on a Harley Davidson. She often imagined him as the dashing hero. He would whisk her back to his castle; or escort her to a glamorous night at the theater. She kissed it for the millionth time and responded to her heart covered duvet, as it called her in for the night.

Thanks to her mom. She was knowledgeable on most things, but relationship advice hadn't been on the agenda. Mia missed out on forming close friends after being home-schooled in a quiet neighborhood. She'd only made a few friends growing up, getting to know each other, when their moms met for a coffee. In their sheltered lives, it gave them friendly contact, but they didn't form the deep connection Mia craved.

As the years went by, their contact diminished further. Mia had the occasional chat over the phone hearing of their exploits, but she had nothing exciting to report. Mia's chance of meeting a lad who'd commit to forming a proper relationship grew more difficult with the advancements of sexbots.

The intelligent droids gave the guys everything they wanted, from great sex, to cooking and cleaning for them. Mia's parents got their own house droid to do the chores whilst Mia studied with her mom. Tyler was not a sexbot though. That would have spiked the arguments past breaking point.

Chapter 2

Home was a modest detached, on which became a quiet street. Their solid oak door, the only evidence of their Devonshire roots. It set their house apart from the modern renewables around them, occupied by private people who never left their home. Most had moved into the nearby climate-controlled city to avoid the storms. The only glimpse of life, an occasional face peeking out to watch service robots collect the rubbish. Mia also liked to watch as the wind sometimes blew them over. The robots just got up and carried on regardless, their war of attrition both humorous to see, whilst also a great lesson for life.

The only evidence of a loving relationship in Mia's life was her parents. Her dad, Gary, was a sturdy, hard-working technical manager and her mom, Ferne, was his first love, a delicate little lady with model-like features. Whenever he came home, she would run to the front door to greet him. They would hold each other tight, kissing in a passionate embrace as if he'd been away for months. After their embrace, he would let her put her feet up as he fetched and carried for her, before they would snuggle together and watch an old movie.

Over the years, their relationship changed. He came home

much later, and she no longer ran to him. He would still go to her, but the long hugs became shorter and shorter until polite pecks replaced them. For the last year, he'd gone to Mia instead. He hugged her so hard sometimes she feared her bones would crush under his powerful arms, but she still enjoyed the feel of his love. The hugs recently were different. It seemed like he wasn't giving her a hug but was trying to hold on to a life drifting away from him.

Dad finally relented to mom's constant request to buy her a little coffee shop, which she'd dreamt about since her child-hood. He used the money he'd been putting aside for his retirement and prioritized, making her dream a reality instead.

He'd planned to give up work, so they could run it together. However, she did the numbers and said they still needed the money from his job. Perhaps it was true, but she needed her own space and identity more. She said Mia could help instead, so they upgraded Tyler to do the remaining chores at home, whilst they got to work on the new family business.

Mia and her mom worked together to update the coffee shop. They threw the old plastic chairs out and bought some to their own design. Mia and her mom sat in front of the screen for an age, mulling over the leather and thread color. They agreed on decorative yellow stitching on red leather cushions with matching squabs for their chrome framed chairs.

When dad found out how much they'd spent, he complained they were spending too much. Mom vocalized her frustration in another of their mini squabbles, but when the chairs arrived, they agreed they were superb.

Mia matched the shopfront in primrose yellow with a brush script font in red for the sign written name, Mom & Mia's. It sat in-between a charity shop and a hearing center in a small arcade, protected from the storms and the baking temperatures. The coffee shop was opposite a tanning salon which had closed, when the fashion for paler skin had a run.

They upgraded the air conditioning to premium, to trickle oxygen through to their grateful customers. The higher air quality made it an instant hit with the elderly residents. On most days they'd come in for a drink, a chat, and a welcome break from their Oxy sticks. Oxy sticks provided oxygen to keep them safe whilst outside. The elderly who couldn't afford the premium air conditioning also depended on them in their homes. The coffee shop allowed the Oxy sticks to get tucked away whilst they could sit, relax and chat over a coffee.

Mia would study in the back and bake cakes, whilst her mom would entertain the regulars. Sometimes, she'd send Mia home, whilst she'd prepare the coffee shop for the next day. When her mom returned home, she'd shun her dad's advances, supposedly worn out from her day's toil. As she became later still, both Mia and her dad had often retired for the night. With mom hardly about, dad engrossed himself more in his work.

It often left Mia alone at home with Tyler, her only company. Tyler's latest update had made him more sociable. He now had softer features and a caring smile and was not much taller than Mia at around five foot eight. They designed him that way, easy on the eye and unimposing. It also ensured a smoother acceptance. When Mia had got used to his upgrade, she invited him to sit with her to watch old films together. Tyler obliged and enjoyed the growing bond between them.

One night, after Tyler had gone to charge, Mia got bored flicking through the multitude of channels and headed back to the coffee shop to help her mom. The short taxi ride enabled her to avoid getting soaked as it dropped her off at the opening to the arcade. As she walked up the arcade, the lights to the coffee shop were off, apart from a light in the kitchen. Mia figured her mom would most likely be reviewing the accounts.

Before she could knock on the door, her mom appeared with her blouse wide open. She ran past the counter, followed by a strong-looking young man with his shirt gaping. Unaware of Mia at the door, they continued to chase each other around, with chairs and tables being strewn about. He caught her and pinned her against the wall. He pulled her head to the side and kissed her neck. She didn't struggle, but she tugged at his shirt. He took it off to reveal his sculptured back. She placed both hands on his chest, before taking him by the hand, leading him back into the kitchen.

It was crystal clear what was happening. Mia left without disturbing them and walked to the end of the arcade. Although stunned by what she had seen, she stopped before the curtain of heavy rain and messaged a taxi.

The emotion welled up inside her as she entered the taxi. When she arrived home, she burst through the door, knocking over a wedding picture on a small table at the foot of the stairs. It was a picture of her parents on Exmouth beach. The words at the base of the frame read 'forever', but the bond between the couple, as with the beach, had gone. She darted to the safety of her bedroom, as the effect of what she'd seen took hold.

Was this a regular thing? Were the late nights bullshit so she could fraternize with another man? Did her dad know? What would happen if he knew? What would happen to Mia?

If she told her dad, all hell would break loose. It was best to say nothing. She shouldn't get involved.

The next night, her mom was late again. Was it a one-off, or did she love someone else? If her mom was happier, it could be a good thing for her, if not for Mia and her dad. When Mia arrived outside the coffee shop, more in hope than expectation, her heart pulled again. Her mom, who'd taught her right from wrong. Who'd cuddled her when she came home from another disappointing date, was with yet another Man. Her mom was bent over the counter, skirt hitched up to her waist. It was crystal clear what was happening.

Mia's heart fell as she turned away, walking home in the driving rain. With each step, her previously stable world crumbled. The life she'd experienced to date faded further from her idealistic love stories. Her adult life had hardly begun, but she didn't care for it. Drenched throughout, sapped of mental and physical energy, she rested under a bridge sheltering from the rain. Mia tried to make sense of it, but to no avail. She hugged her legs to keep warm, but a chill grabbed her. As a depression took over her, she considered her pointless, loveless life.

A dark figure approached. She trembled equally with cold and fear. If this was to be her end? Did she even care? She hesitantly glanced up at the sinister dark hood. As he pulled back his hood, the evil she expected to see merely revealed a mature man with a kind face. When he spoke, her eyes lifted to him, and her mind opened.

He said calmly but firmly, "It's not time to give up, only the Lord decides when. It doesn't matter what has brought you to this point, get yourself back on your feet and go again. Joys you've not experienced yet, are closer than you think. Make sure you don't miss them."

The correct response should have been to thank him for his kind-spirited words. It seemed every word would be with her forever, to push her on when things were hard. As his words sank in, he pulled his hood forward and disappeared again into the rain, before Mia responded with a late shout of, "thank you!"

Fresh from his words, she reached for her phone; her shaking fingers messaged an autonomous taxi. Gladly, it arrived almost instantly. She stepped in and apologized for her sodden state, not that a physical driver was there to complain. It was only a two-minute journey, but the emotions of the last two evenings had stripped her resolve, the kind words of the stranger, the only thing holding her together. She felt a warmth return as the taxi rolled in front of their familiar oak door. Tyler opened it and stepped into the rain to help her into the house.

Tyler closed the door behind her. "You should get in the shower and get warm."

"Okay," Mia said, and she trudged slowly up the stairs.

"Are you okay?" Tyler asked.

Mia mumbled, "fantastic."

When she reached the top of the stairs, she assured Tyler she would be okay and headed straight for the en-suite. The warming needles revitalized her soul and cleared her troubled mind. Telling her dad would be a bad idea, despite her mom's behavior. She needed to talk to her. Perhaps it was a phase she was going through, and everything would turn out okay.

The following day, Mia tried to discuss the previous night with her mom, but she avoided the subject. Mia became more aware as she noticed the same pattern continue. More men would appear at the coffee shop door before they disappeared without ordering. She would again stay late.

A few nights later, when her dad arrived home, his usual callout to Mia was missing. He didn't close the door correctly, and the wind blew it back against its hinges. Mia went to him and gave him a strong cuddle to lift his spirits. The hug he returned was even stronger, which caused Mia to give out a pained yelp. He stopped instantly and headed upstairs without a word. Mia watched him go, wanting to follow him but also relieved to get out of his powerful grasp.

Tyler slipped past her and closed the door before putting a comforting arm around her. Mia wanted to go to her dad but opted for the safer option of Tyler's more controlled touch.

Something had frustrated him, but as usual, he didn't vocalize his feelings. Mia thanked Tyler and crept upstairs. Her dad was grunting and mumbling in his bedroom, so she quietly changed and settled into bed.

Her mom was still not home, late even by her standards. As the storm lashed heavier around the house, a crack sounded loud through the night, followed by a thud. Mia went to her window to investigate. The tree from next door had crashed into their back garden.

Her dad seemed oblivious, until he stormed through from his bedroom, hurried downstairs and headed straight out the door. Mia assumed he would assess the damage. His mind was, however, focused on other damage as he jumped into a taxi. He must have gone to the coffee shop. Maybe he'd worked out what was happening.

Ten minutes later, he arrived back alone, striding upstairs. She heard him knocking things about in his office. Mia guessed what must have happened. She wanted to talk to him, but the bangs in the office told her the red mist had descended and sensibly she kept away. She drowned out the ongoing storm both inside and out, with dreamy love songs.

Chapter 3

The storms had ceased and Mia awoke to a peaceful house, lazily stretching in the warmth of her bed.

Her mom finally arrived home. She opened the door expecting a volley of abuse, but all was quiet. She shouted hello, even when she came back late, but the later she got the quieter she became. This morning, she crept in like a mouse. The only sound was the creaking door and the short squeak on the seventh step. Mia called out to her, and she came to her room. She gave Mia a nervous smile before she glanced behind her.

"What's going on?" Mia asked.

"I've met someone else. I need to talk to your dad."

Mia wanted to scream but said nothing. She held her breath, digging her nails into her own arm.

Her mom left to face him. With apprehension, she entered their bedroom, then the office, before she ran downstairs.

"Where's your dad?" she shouted back up to Mia.

"I don't know!"

She ran back up to the bedroom and checked the drawers in the office. "Where are the bank cards?"

Mia's anger spilt over, screeching out, "I don't blame him, you fucking whore!"

She ran back into her daughter's bedroom. "Don't speak to

me like that!"

Mia cowered with her mom's hand about to strike, but she stopped as Mia said, "I've seen you at the coffee shop!"

The color in her mom's face turned pale, "You didn't tell your dad, did you?"

"I didn't have to, he worked it out himself."

"Where's he gone?" the dawning of the moment and the effect hit her all at once.

Mia sighed, "I don't know."

Her mom twitched as her mind spun. "Can you open the coffee shop?"

"I suppose so," Mia's redundant response.

"Thanks," she said before she headed back downstairs.

Mia could hear her speaking to Tyler but struggled to make out the detail. Mia headed to the shower, hoping to clear her head. She should stay strong for her; despite the way she's behaved. They will have to stick together, whatever happens. She rested her head against the glass door of the shower as the hot jets massaged away at the torment in her head.

As the darkness lifted, she caught her hand on one of the tile edges. Her dad had built the en-suite, so she could have her own privacy. She stroked the imperfections and remembered when she helped him lay the tiles. He used to call them the three amigos. They'd had such fun times, but with her parents' bond broken, the good times were unlikely to return.

Mia stepped out the shower with a clearer mind. A shower always brought her some clarity. After wrapping a warm beach towel around her delicate frame, she stepped back into her bedroom. A door slammed and Mia called out to her mom. There was no reply. She dried off and made her way downstairs to find Tyler preparing breakfast.

"Where's my mom?"

Tyler replied in a formal tone, "Your mom left three minutes ago, with two suitcases. A gentleman collected her. I do not know their destination. She left these for you," Tyler presented her the keys for the coffee shop.

"Where's my dad?"

"Your Father left nine hours, thirty-four mins ago. He took a suitcase, a bag, and his laptop."

"What am I supposed to do now?" Mia looked to Tyler for support.

"I will always be here for you," Tyler said, not giving her the formal response she'd expected.

"Thanks, Tyler." She hugged him. He responded, wrapping his arms around her. She tightened her grip against his firm exterior, and he returned a firmer squeeze. His powerful arms around her delivered her to a more reassuring and comfortable place.

Tyler had always been there for Mia. Over the years the clunky helping hand, who'd picked up after her when she was younger, had grown with her. Tyler also developed and berated her for dropping things on the floor, as she'd done it on purpose, attempting to wind him up.

Tyler had become a good friend, offering advice and boosting her confidence with compliments on her appearance. His sympathetic ear, always ready to listen as he learned how to be more human, improving himself and the network.

Tyler released his arms. "That was nice, but I suggest you get dressed. Mom & Mia's is due to open in forty-six minutes and you do not want to be late for your first day in charge." Tyler's informative style was more relaxed than she'd noticed before. She liked the change.

Mia put her hand on Tyler's shoulder, "Thanks for the hug," then she strode upstairs with a renewed vigor.

To be able to run the coffee shop had Mia excited, but she needed to look the part. She looked through several options, then headed into her mom's room. She selected a frilly white blouse but noticed a button missing. Mia remembered when her mom had worn it last and threw it to the floor. The memory of her mom bent over the counter would never leave her mind, no matter how many showers she had.

Mia looked through more dresses before she selected a white dress with red polka dots and lace trim. It was the outfit her mom had worn the day the coffee shop opened, so it made an excellent choice for Mia's first day in charge.

Mia had opened the shop before, when her mom's legs were aching. She'd needed to stay in bed for a few days. Her mom had a rare condition, claudication, which caused severe pain in her legs. It rarely affected her, but when the pain came, she needed to rest. She declined the revascularization procedure to fix the issue, giving her dad short thrift when he'd suggested amputation for robot legs. Instead, she did her stretching exercises and other than an issue two months ago, she'd been fine for three years.

Opening the coffee shop was different this time. As she approached, she paused and looked at the shopfront, Mom & Mia's. She remembered picking the font for the sign-writer with her mom and everything was bright, but now the paint on the shopfront looked jaded. The friendly ambiance remained with soft shades, a warm welcome, and the pleasant slideshow on the back wall.

Aside from interruptions for the news, the slideshow transitioned through green fields, sunsets, homely cottages and sandy beaches with waves breaking on the shore. Mia had wanted a larger screen, but her mom said it would intrude when the image changed. They agreed on the smaller screen, pleasant to watch but discreet enough not to impose itself on the customers. Mia chose two gray-scale pictures for either side of the screen.

Mia looked through the door whilst she struggled with the key in the lock. Some chairs were still out of place, bringing back the image of her mom and her sexual acquaintances. Why did she go sex-mad? Why couldn't she stay happy with dad? Mia looked at the gray-scale images on the wall. They were more poignant than ever. The one on the left showed a woodland path. It echoed the journey they began when they opened the coffee shop and also portrayed the journey everyone must take. To walk along the uneven path of life, not knowing where it will lead, like her own future.

Her favorite picture on the right had an old couple in silhouette. They were hand in hand, strolling along the beach. It portrayed a peaceful image of love that stood the test of time. When the coffee shop fell quiet, she often imagined being in the picture with a love of her own. Today, it merely reminded her how her parents had left her alone.

She switched on the slideshow and put the chairs in their correct places. She vocalized her frustration to the empty coffee shop. "Why did she mess things up? Dad adores her... and all for sex... she must be crazy!"

With her parents both gone. She'd be left to run the coffee shop alone and would therefore have to deal with potential suitors herself. Her chances of finding love would stand a better chance when she wasn't hiding away in the kitchen.

Chapter 4

An old couple came in for their daily fresh air and coffee boost. They asked about her mom, but Mia brushed it off, saying she'd be back tomorrow. It struck Mia, she'd been in the coffee shop for five years, albeit mainly in the kitchen, but had never chatted with them. The friendly looking couple sat taking in the filtered oxygen as Mia prepared their coffees.

With no one else in, she took them their drinks and asked if she could join them for a while. They introduced themselves as Pete and Paulina; it seemed like many old couples; they shared the first letter of their names. Maybe that's why her parents, Gary and Ferne didn't last. After some small talk, she asked them how they'd met. After a short discussion, Pete accepted it was the nightclub and not at the local bar. Paulina reminded him how she'd bumped into him. She'd been gazing at his cheeky face without a response.

"I thought I'd bumped into you," Pete replied.

"He was a gentleman," Paulina continued, "he insisted on buying me a drink. We chatted away until his favorite song came on and he asked me to join him for a dance. The dance floor was full, so he spent most of the song putting his arms out to stop anyone bumping into me."

"I wanted to protect my little angel," he said, as he reached over and stroked her shoulder.

"You made me feel like I was the only girl there," Paulina added.

"From that moment you were." His loving gaze changed to a cheeky grin, "The drugs you slipped in my drink worked. I was a right lad before I met you."

Paulina turned to Mia, "He's been cracking that joke for sixty years. When he protected me, I knew I'd found a man who'd look after me."

"Have you got yourself a fella?" Pete inquired.

Mia sighed, trying to appear nonchalant, "Tried them and didn't like it."

They both reassured her a fella would arrive when she least expected it as she got up to greet another couple. Mia helped them take a seat whilst taking their order. They wanted her favorite lemon drizzle cakes. Mia sorted their order, before returning to the kitchen to check on the next batch.

Despite it being a busy morning, Mia chatted with most of the couples, hearing their romantic stories about how they'd met. David and Deb were a good-looking older couple, who'd returned from another trip to Mars to visit their son, Jack. David recounted, "Jack always wanted to be a spaceman, running around the house, flying his rocket. We're so proud of him, living his dream and working in space." David showed Mia a recent picture, "A good-looking guy, an engineer, a fine catch for any girl."

"Is he single?" Mia enquired.

"Is he single!" Deb laughed, "His only vice is women, he has a different girl every time we see him."

"Typical bloke, all the good-looking ones are gay or they want to have sex with every woman on the planet."

"It's why he moved to Mars, he'd been with all the girls on earth," David quipped.

Deb slapped his arm and protested, "It's not something to be proud of," she turned to Mia, "I wish he'd settle down."

"He's still young, let him have his fun," David added.

"He's thirty-five, he should get married and settle down," Deb said.

"Still looking for the right one, I suppose. Are you single, Mia?"

"Yep, happy to be, at the minute anyway." She made her excuses and returned to check the cakes.

Mia removed a new batch from the oven. She imagined a small boy running around, "Watch out, these are hot."

The imaginary boy asked, "Can I have one?"

She responded, "When they're cooler Darling, they'd burn your little fingers now."

"Okay Mommy," was his reply as he turned tail and ran the opposite way, vanishing as a tentative voice came from inside the coffee shop.

"Excuse me, can we pay now?" Pete said with Paulina by his side. They'd sat taking in the air for about an hour after they finished their coffees.

As they turned to leave, Paulina whispered, "You'll make a great mom, one day."

Mia blushed as she stood behind the counter. She smiled and waved as they eventually closed the door behind them. David and Deb were still debating their son's shenanigans. She left them to it and straightened the chairs. Another couple was also getting ready to leave, so she helped them with their coats. They took some deep breaths before heading on their way. David and Deb were not far behind them, which left leave Mia alone for a break.

Mia enjoyed a coffee and a slice of cake. The only sound was from the air conditioning humming its familiar tune. It was during the quiet moments in the shop, when her mom shared recordings of when Mia was little. Mia replayed her mom holding out her hands as she took her first steps. Her mom caught her as she fell into her arms, before lifting her high in the air. Mia's mobile burst into life, taking her out of her reflective bliss. It was a pleasant surprise, a call from her dad.

"Hiya Darling, just arrived in Shenyang."

"You could have told me you were leaving. Why are you in China?"

"I don't do soppy goodbyes."

Her dad explained how work had become more and more stressful with the Chinese plant's awful quality performance. His boss told him to go to China and sort it out. When he went to talk to her mom to discuss it, he saw her with another man. So, he returned home and planned his China assignment and moved credits into a new account.

A few nights later, he'd cooled off and wanted to talk to her again, only to spot someone else at the shop with her. Despite his strength, he wasn't a violent man. He'd tried so hard to please her, but the harder he tried, the less she responded. He stopped paying into her account to get a reaction, but nothing. She was occupied elsewhere and when he came home to say he had to leave for China; she was missing again.

With trepidation or more likely painful expectation, he went again to the coffee shop. To see his wife, happy in the arms of yet another lover. Many men would have snapped, smashed the window, screamed, or at least confronted her. He just turned away and returned home. Back home, he cleared all the accounts, grabbed what he needed and left without a word.

He apologized for not telling Mia he had to go, "I should have told you. I'm only here for about three months. We can sort your mom out, when I get back."

Mia apologized to her dad, "I knew. I should have told you."

"It's not your fault!"

Resting her head on her hand, Mia let out a sigh, "Mom's gone too." She recounted the morning's events to her dad.

"I can send some money, if you need any."

Mia stared through her glistening eyes at her half-empty coffee cup. "It's not money I need. It's you." Her telltale sniffle pulled at his heart.

Saddened to hear his daughter upset, yet unable to help, he made his excuse to end the call, "Sorry Darling, I've got to go now, love you, bye."

Mia sobbed alone for a few minutes. It shattered the cozy world she knew. Her protective father in another land and her Mother who said she'd always be there for her, was in another man's arms.

Her own love life deemed never to even start and her best friend, a robot. With her arms soaked by her sorrow, the doorbell rang. The door tentatively opened and a tall, well-dressed young man stood in the doorway. He asked, "Is Ferne about?"

Her sorrow turned to rage, "No! She's not!" Mia storming to the door, "Get lost and don't come back here!" she slammed the door behind him as he fled.

She wiped away her tears, trembling with adrenaline, with the image of him and her mom together. As she calmed down, she wondered if he'd been some innocent guy she'd yelled at.

She smiled to herself, proud and surprised she'd scared him enough for him to run away.

Still pleased with herself, she called her friend Ellie. Mia hadn't shouted at anybody before, even Ben, who'd turned her image of love into a nightmare. Ellie listened but was almost bursting when Mia asked her if she had any news.

Given Mia's troubles, she held back on the details but told her she'd been on a few dates with Connor. Connor was their marijuana delivery lad; he'd proved to be quite a gentleman. She added they were a good fit for each other, and the sex was awesome. Ellie held off the fuller details for a better time and asked Mia, "Shall I introduce you to Connor's friend."

Mia declined, "No Thanks. My life's enough of a tornado already. Men can wait for a while."

Mia had grown up with three friends, Kat, Lucy and Ellie. Kat was her bestie, what a girl, a truly wild child, bronze skin, dark brown wavy locks, with deep dark brown mesmerizing eyes. Kat's mom home-schooled her to protect everyone else, rather than protecting her daughter.

Lucy similar to Mia had a small, slender frame. She was rather reserved, but smart and studious. She would try to get the other girls to focus on their task, but Kat always put a playful spin on it.

Ellie was an entirely different proposition, full of confidence and always the prettiest. She grew into a tall blond, with the shape and elegance to turn any guy's head. She would usually go along with whatever the moms had given them. However, Ellie surprised them, when one day she'd produced a bullet vibrator from her study bag. Ellie had tickled her nose with it. Before she passed it to Mia. Mia did likewise and shook her head at the unwelcome tickle. She didn't know its real purpose until she handed it to Kat.

Kat slid it between her legs and wriggled her body, making some fake moaning noises, before she'd laughed and handed it to Lucy. Lucy appeared mortified, but little did the others know she already had her own sex toy. It had been a joke gift from her brother Ryan. Lucy had thought it was a model of a dick until she checked online and found out its real purpose. She had no intention of trying it. But she'd tentatively switched it on and shrieked at the frightening sight of it as it had wriggled on her bed. She summoned the courage and grabbed it, switched it off and hid it in the back of a cupboard.

Chapter 5

Mid-afternoon and the doorbell went to signify break time was over, as Ray clunked through. She'd talked to Ray before, he'd been housebound for many years, cared for by his wife Ria. When she passed away, he got a life assurance pay-out which paid for an exoskeleton which enabled him to get back on his feet. Ray, now fully mobile, enjoyed every day, getting out with his friends. Most afternoons he would come to Mom & Mia's. Every time becoming cheekier, forever cracking jokes and light-heartedly offering himself as a willing suitor for Mia.

Next through the door was Sarah. A quiet, sturdy lady who knew Ray's late wife, Ria. Sarah had introduced them to the coffee shop. Her daughter was a friend of Ferne who'd encouraged them to visit and they'd soon become familiar with Mia's lemon drizzle cake.

Harry and Jackie came in to complete the crew. Harry was Ray's best friend, a small rather studious gent with his wife Jackie, a fun-loving lady, who liked Ray and his humorous chat.

Ray and his crew were the perfect tonic for Mia. They chatted about everything, from the crazy weather, to the latest news and techniques for Mia to find the right man. Today, the news covered the growing popularity of the Tushi sexbots and the recent change in the law. People could now marry them.

The Tushi bots were the creation of genius, Okzu Tushi and his Tushi Corporation. Tushi had the market share for both sexbots and the humble housebots. Mia's housebot Tyler was a Tushi creation too. Whilst the crew had concerns with the sudden rise of the Tushi bots. They conceded that they were fulfilling a societal need, despite taking away the old-fashioned values of human to human courtship.

Mia defended the rise of the robots and the good they had done. "The roads are much safer since autonomous vehicles took over." She continued, "And my house bot, Tyler is fantastic. He does all the household chores and is a super cook." Mia continued, "courtship and romance may be in decline, but they are not dead yet. Ellie's dating a regular guy."

Jackie quipped, "Makes a nice change from all the people calling Robo-Dick or Fanny-Annie."

Harry offered words of caution, "Romantics are a dying breed. Mia, you shouldn't be too choosy."

"I'm still waiting," Ray smiled as he opened his arms wide.

Mia gave a quick-witted response, "Someone under fifty and willing to talk to me about something other than sex is not choosy." She patted Ray on the shoulder, opting not to go for another cuddle.

"You'll find a guy," Ray said.

"Thanks, RoboCop," Mia joked at Ray in his exoskeleton suit.

After Ray and his friends had gone, Mia cleaned up with a fresh spring in her step. As she caught the short ride home, she thought about Ellie. She was pleased for her friend, yet saddened at her own dormant love life.

Perhaps she should call Ellie back and meet Connor's friend. She opted instead to call Kat and repeated her tale of woe. Mia added how Ellie had made progress with Connor and mentioned she should go out with his friend.

Kat interrupted Mia's flow, "Aaron!"

"She didn't mention his name."

"I dated Connor's Mate, Aaron, for a few weeks. He's good in bed, but he's wasted on pot most of the time. You don't need a guy like Aaron."

"I hope Connor's not a druggie," said Mia, concerned for the smitten Ellie.

"Connor! He's switched on. Plus, great looks and a fit body to match, definitely a keeper, Ellie's a lucky bitch."

"Need me, one of those," Mia quipped, her hand squeezing some imaginary fella's bum.

"Thought you'd given up on love?"

"I can always try again, maybe an older guy," Mia said.

Kat replied in an instant, "I will get on 4-Sum Date. It has older, more measured guys. Less bull at a gate than the youngsters."

"Sounds interesting, as long as they don't just want me for sex," Mia remembering her last dating episode and how vulnerable she felt.

"You're a good-looking woman, they're blokes, they'll want sex," Kat said matter of fact like, "but it's up to you, as always."

Mia agreed, "Okay, I suppose it will be good to get out."

"I'll get right on it," Kat ended the call and set about organizing everything.

Fifteen minutes later, Kat called back with an update. "We're on for later, I've reserved a table. We've got Mirek, he's thirty-three and Ethan's thirty-two."

"That was quick. What do they look like?"

"Mirek is tall, dark and handsome. Ethan's a little cuddly but he's cute and has a friendly face, he'll be fun. We are meeting them in town. The taxi will collect us at seven o'clock to meet at Giangolini's, the Italian Place. I'll come around about half-past six. I can help you pick something to wear."

Mia squeezed out an Okay before Kat rang off.

Kat was a treasure, but also a whirlwind. Once Kat had an idea in her head, she was always laser focussed. Mia would have preferred to look through the profile pictures but had got railroaded in a blur of Kat-ness.

She pondered as the tornado in her head settled; It's a meal out, it gets me out the house and Kat's there for backup. Mia recalled the last time she ventured out with Kat; she didn't help much. Kat had met a guy, and after an hour dancing together they disappeared.

Mia searched for her in the club, but to no avail. When she called her, Kat was in a taxi with a guy, heading to his place. It left Mia alone to fend off the hungry wolves. When approached by two big muscular guys, she got scared and rushed into the ladies.

She stayed in there for an hour before she darted out and grabbed a taxi home. Kat had been apologetic and said she'd looked across and seen a guy talking to her and assumed she was okay for the night.

Kat assured Mia she wouldn't leave her alone again.

Chapter 6

Mirek appeared at Ethan's desk to confirm plans for their night out. They'd been best mates for twenty years and shared accommodation when they first moved to the Midlands from Manchester.

Mirek launched his own marketing company and it was doing well. Unfortunately, he took in one employee too many. The beauty he then promoted to be his wife. They divorced just two years later. Ethan had feared as much when Mirek fell for the immaculate gold digger.

Mirek sold his business, partly for the divorce pay off, but mainly due to the stress of the divorce. He wished he had taken Ethan's advice and kept well away.

A few months later, Ethan spotted a vacancy at the Tushi Corporation. Ethan used his influence and got an interview for his friend. The following week, Mirek joined his buddy at the biggest employer in the country.

Ethan had been with the Tushi Corporation for ten years and was one of their most well-respected engineers. Despite his immense success with design and development, he'd not made much progress on the love front, so he volunteered to test out the new AI Tushi girls. He'd been working on them, so it made sense to take his work home for his own pleasure.

Mirek had also assisted with the testing. Perfect figures were the norm for him, whether sexbot or human. But having had his fill of Tushi girls, he convinced Ethan they should try real women for a change and signed them up with the new 4-Sum date app. Ethan agreed, figuring it could be fun or good research.

"Be good to get you back into dating," Mirek declared.

"I suppose you're right," Ethan replied

"I'm looking forward to the challenge," Mirek added.

Ethan looked at his taller leaner buddy, "challenge? Body-swap with me for the night? That would be a challenge!"

Mirek smiled at his buddy as he clapped his hands around his own firm stomach. "You have the cuddle factor, you'll be fine."

Ethan shrugged and with an open-handed gesture replied, "It's a No! to the body-swap then."

"Not even Okzu Tushi can do that."

* * *

With no more customers about Mia's imaginary little boy appeared again, "Are we going to make more cakes?"

"Not today son, we can make some tomorrow."

"Someone else is coming in," he said, pointing to the door.

Mia glanced at the door as a smooth, handsome face peered through the window.

Mia turned back to the boy, "You can help with some icing tomorrow." The boy vanished as the click of the door broke their private moment.

The smart-looking chap, perhaps in his early thirties, opened the door; he wore a navy double-breasted suit and with his short trim fair hair looked like a salesman. He paused with the door ajar and politely asked, "Hi Mia, are you still open?"

It was rare anyone came after four, but she did often leave for home around that time. A little flushed, she cleared her throat and composed herself trying to sound calm, "About to close, but you can have a coffee if you like?"

A smile came on his face, "black, one sugar please," and he closed the door behind him. As he approached the counter, he pointed to the last slice of lemon drizzle cake, "Did you save the last slice for me?"

"You can have it if you like," Mia replied nonchalantly as she made him his coffee.

"Yes please," his eager reply.

As she passed him his coffee, his eyes fixed on hers. She sensed it and looked away. Mia grabbed the cake plate and passed it without catching his gaze.

She expected him to take a seat, but he stood at the counter. "They are lovely chairs, have a seat."

He took a seat nearest to the counter, "Good idea! Would you like to join me?"

"No thanks!", she sniped back, "I'm not like my mom."

He looked perplexed by her sharp retort and fell quiet for a minute as he stared into his drink.

Mia busied herself yet wondered if she'd offended him. She'd assumed him to be another of her mom's men, but he hadn't mentioned her.

She felt the need to break the silence she'd created but remained skeptical, "Have you been here before?"

He had just taken a bite of his cake, so he raised his hand, pointing to his mouthful. Before he replied, "Yes, a long time ago."

"How did you know my name was Mia?" She continued to

probe.

"The Coffeeshop name is a bit of a giveaway," his witty reply, putting Mia more at ease.

"Do you know my mom?"

"Was she the older woman working here?" he asked.

"Yes, would have been my mom."

"The reins all yours now?" he casually questioned.

"Yep," Mia lightened to him, "Well, you know my name, but I don't know yours."

He stood and put out his right hand like a formal business introduction, "Andy Taylor, pleased to meet you." He clenched her hand. His strong hands could have crushed hers, but he had a tender control to his touch.

"Pleased to meet you, Mr. Taylor," she smiled as she looked into his blue eyes.

He returned a smile, "Call me Andy."

She playfully stayed formal, holding her frame straight and tall, "Thank you for coming to my coffee shop, Andy Taylor." She reached forward and took his empty plate before adding in a friendlier tone, "Now can you finish your coffee? I want to close up."

"No problem," he replied before he finished it. Andy passed the cup to Mia, and she cradled the warm cup in her hands as he settled with the payment machine. He thanked Mia for the drink and when he got to the door, he switched the sign to closed and smiled, "Nice to meet you, see you again."

"Hope so," Mia replied, as he closed the door behind him. She continued, "you're always welcome for another coffee," but realized the last words he would have heard were, "hope so," with the image of her still holding his cup.

The little boy appeared again and asked, "Why were your

cheeks red when he talked to you?" The boy continued, "Did you like him?"

It had been nice to see someone nearer her age.

"He was a pleasant customer, that's all. When you run a business, you should be nice to everyone, even the good-looking ones."

Mia gave him a smile as he floated away like a cherub through the ceiling. After closing the coffee shop, she headed home, with a touch more spring in her step and looking forward to her night out.

Mia picked out a selection for Kat to help her choose; Jeans and a white tee-shirt with a retro Jean jacket, her little black dress with a red shawl, a floral dress or maybe leggings and a long cozy gray jumper. Her mobile buzzed into life with a video call from her mom.

"How'd it go?" her mom asked.

"Okay, fairly quiet." Mia added with a smile, "I told one of your fancy men to get lost though."

She laughed before asking, "What did he look like?"

"Didn't catch much of him. He ran off. A tall thin bloke with messy brown hair."

Her mom checked behind herself and whispered, "It would have been Daniel. He'd be good for you. He's a gentle lover."

Mia said, "I'm not interested in going out with any guys you've tested out. Anyway, he's too tall." The image of your parents having sex is gross enough. Having seen her mom in the act with another fella, was worse.

Her mom ignored her disgust and teased, "There are benefits of being with a tall guy."

Mia interrupted, "I'm more interested in why you've taken off and left me on my own."

"I'm sorry, Darling. I was in a panic this morning." She continued, "I'm staying with Dave, he's always been my favorite and he wanted me to move in with him."

"Will you be in the coffee shop tomorrow? I'm having a night out with Kat and two fellas."

Her mom avoided the question and teased, "Finally, getting out for some sex."

Mia snapped back, "Not everyone is as sex-mad as you, it's a pleasant evening at Giangolini's."

"Must be rich to be taking you to Giangolini's. It'll be worth it." She smiled before adding, "for a foursome."

"Mom! That's disgusting."

Her mom giggled as Mia recoiled at such a thought.

Mia stared at her through the screen and asked again, "Are you opening the shop tomorrow?"

"No, I transferred the ownership to you this morning. It's all yours now. Tyler has the details."

"I thought we were running it together." Mia replied, before she asked, "Are you coming back home?"

Her mom answered, "It's time for me to move on. You're a big girl now. You can take care of yourself."

"But Mom" she pleaded.

"Mia, Darling. It's best this way." She glanced over her shoulder, "I've got to go, see you soon, love you."

As the phone died, Mia screamed out her frustration and buried her face in her pillow.

Tyler bounded upstairs and glanced around the door, "Are you okay?" Mia didn't answer, but Tyler had heard the conversation and reassured her, "I will never leave you."

Mia spoke through the pillow, "Thanks, Tyler."

Tyler went downstairs to continue his chores. He'd been a

steady influence in her life. He first arrived as a basic cleaning bot. But after several upgrades, Tyler looked more human and was more like a friendly butler than a housebot.

Tyler was the steady influence on the family. Her dad had moody moments. Her mom would either be dancing and singing around the house or shouting at everything that moved. Tyler, however, was always friendly; he never complained, and he'd always be there. He not only did the housework but provided friendship and emotional support to Mia.

With her parents gone, Mia needed Tyler more than ever.

Chapter 7

A joyful rapping on the door announced Kat's arrival. Tyler opened it and greeted her. Kat was rather windswept, but it was her style. She strode past Tyler and shouted upstairs to Mia.

Mia heard the door and jumped up, pulling off her blouse and darting into the en-suite. She splashed water over her face to freshen up and replied to Kat's call, "Come up."

Kat burst through the door with her usual energy and poked her head into the en-suite, "Hiya." She caught Mia drying off her face. "Okay, let's get this girl ready." Kat spoke confidently to Mia, ignoring the obvious touch of despair in Mia's eyes as they returned to the bedroom.

"My mom's not coming back, and my dad's moved to China," Mia said.

Kat was fake sympathetic for a moment, "That's a bummer... . folks are always a let-down." Kat moved on brightly, "We'll stick together, come on!" She clapped, "We have dates to get ready for."

"What should I wear?" Mia pointed to the finalists from her earlier selection.

Kat had moved out from home some years ago, mainly to get

away from her overbearing parents. Now she was living a freer life, enjoying plenty of male attention quoting, "It requires many frogs to find a prince." She was, however, getting fed up with the frogs.

After her bad experience, Mia followed a slower course, keeping away from boys for the last year. However, she figured it was time to get herself out and meet guys again. Mia was holding onto the hope that the romantic experiences from movies and books would someday come alive for her.

Kat stepped into compare mode as she took each selection in her hand, draping it across herself. "Well ladies and gentlemen, the first finalist is the classic jeans and white tee-shirt combo, with a short leather jacket. What does this tell us? The lady concerned is classy but doesn't want her prospective partner to think she's trying. The tight clothes show confidence to show her slender legs and the plain white top shows her slim waist and the shape of her breasts."

Mia gave a quick correction, "The jeans are tight to protect me from wandering hands."

Kat laid them onto the bed and swept the little black dress around a few times before presenting it across her ample breasts. "The second selection is the standard outfit for a night out, the little black dress. Show some leg, show a little cleavage. Guaranteed to get you laid."

Mia interjected, "It is a little cleavage compared to yours."

"You can control yours better, my boobs move all over the place," Kat joked around pushing her breasts up and down.

Mia cupped her own breasts and announced, "I'm happy with my smaller boobs."

Kat meanwhile had selected the next wannabe outfit. "The Third outfit is a vintage floral red rose and cream sleeveless dress. It makes a clear statement, she's a classy lady." Kat held it close as she spun around with it, "You can look, but please don't touch me," in her best Sandra Dee voice.

Mia lurched over the bed and grabbed the jeans, "These will do, don't want to look like I'm trying too hard."

Kat agreed it was a good choice, "You can save the little black dress for the second date."

"If there's a second date?"

"There won't be a first date if you don't get a wriggle on."

Mia tipped backward on the bed as pulled her jeans to her waist. She selected a thick leather belt from a drawer and laced it through. Kat checked her make-up in the mirror and touched up her lipstick. Kat also wore jeans with a warm orange sweater. She looked stunning as usual, her matching lipstick framed her perfect smile. Mia put on her top and grabbed her leather jacket, her comfort jacket. Her dad had brought it about three years ago, and whenever she felt nervous, she'd put it on. It was her own little shield. She put on her matching boots and announced, "Ready."

"Do you want some lippy on?" Kat had picked a couple out of her clutch bag.

Mia tilted her head and pondered for a moment before accepting the offer. Mia rarely wore make-up, she occasionally wore lipstick, but didn't bother with all the foundation and eyeliner palaver. She was blessed with nice skin like her mom, so didn't need to cover it.

"Bright red or pink Grapefruit?" Kat asked.

Mia selected, "Pink Grapefruit," and headed back to the mirror.

Kat looked through the mirror at Mia as she applied the lipstick. Kat rested her hands on her shoulders, "It suits you.

The guys are most definitely the lucky ones tonight."

"I hope they behave themselves" Mia picked up some pepper spray from her bedside cupboard, "and I won't have to use this." She dropped it into her small leather clutch bag.

Kat popped into the en-suite. "I need the loo before we go."

"I'll be downstairs."

Tyler gazed at Mia as she descended. "Ravishing," he said before pensively touching his chin, "If only?" Mia responded with a full cheesy smile as she paused on the stairs.

Tyler always made her feel good about herself. As she met him at the foot, she gave him a peck on his cheek, leaving a pink mark. He wished them both well as Kat whisked past. Tyler watched from the door as they entered the awaiting taxi.

He continued to watch as the taxi sped off into the distance and the evening rains began.

* * *

Mirek arrived at Ethan's rather grand home. Perfectly located close to town and the Tushi Corporation, yet far enough away to give him time to work on his next masterpiece. It was what Okzu Tushi had said when he gifted him the house for his outstanding work with the Tushi bots.

As Mirek got out of his car, the front shutter opened. Mirek stood to capture the unhurried shutter unveiling Ethan's latest Tushi sexbot, Chloe. Chloe's red high-heeled shoes appeared first before her slender tanned legs, a delicate short black skirt with white lace trim at the hem and the waist. It exposed her slim bronzed waist next before revealing a white crop top holding in her sizeable assets. Her wavy blond hair framing a near-perfect face, with a beauty spot on her chin, the only

41

blemish. She let him take in her beauty as he approached and gave him a full warming smile.

Chloe swiveled delicately on her toes and called to her lover, "Ethan Darling, Mirek is here."

Chloe was a beauty to behold, but Mirek had experienced enough Tushi girls, like Chloe, and had tired of them. He stepped past her and sauntered along the marble hallway to seek his buddy.

"Hiya Mate, are you ready?"

Ethan shouted from the top of the stairs, "Give me a minute, have a seat in the lounge."

Mirek strolled into the lounge area and took in the main feature. It was the two-meter-long fish tank, with the most beautiful tropical fish.

"Out for a drink with Ethan?" Chloe inquired.

Ethan must have not told her about the double date, so he replied with a simple, "Yep."

"Do you want anything while you wait?" she politely asked.

With his knowledge of the sexbots, Mirek knew she meant anything. He teased her a little, "Yes, please. Could I have a blow job?" as his hand moved over his zip.

"Ethan wouldn't want me to. I was suggesting a drink."

"No Thanks, I'm OK." Mirek turned to re-focus on the fish.

Chloe stood by his side and joined him.

Mirek enquired, "Why do you watch the fish?"

Chloe replied, "People find them relaxing."

"Do you find them relaxing?"

"I am already relaxed. If I have nothing to do, I enjoy watching them swim."

"Can you swim?" he asked, already knowing the answer.

"I am not required to swim."

"Would you like to swim?"

"One Day, perhaps. I think about it when I watch the fish."

Despite being fully aware of the AI developments, Chloe's thought processes surprised Mirek, "I'm sure Ethan could make it happen for you."

"I hope so," Chloe replied.

Mirek and Chloe turned to greet Ethan as he entered the lounge.

"Hiya buddy," Ethan spoke to Mirek as he put his arm around Chloe's waist.

"He asked me for a blow job, but I thought it inappropriate. Should I have obliged your friend?"

"You did the right thing. You should have told him to piss off."

"I would not want to upset your friend."

"You did well". He kissed her on her cheek and signaled to Mirek they should go.

"Have a nice night. I will be ready and waiting when you return," she smiled and followed them to the door.

As they got into the car, Mirek confirmed the pre-set destination and switched it to autonomous so they could chat without the distraction of driving in the rain. Mirek asked Ethan if his Tushi girl knew he was going on a date.

"Got to be kidding. I don't want to upset her," he continued with a jovial tone, "She's my fall-back plan if these girls aren't up for it."

"I said these were classy girls. We must wine and dine them before taking them to mine for some action."

"I suppose, it will make a change to chat first."

Mirek confirmed, "We will have to work for it, take it nice and easy, be the perfect gentlemen."

"You mean play it old school."

"That's always the best way," Mirek replied.

"How was your chat with Chloe?"

"She said she wanted to go swimming. She seems much smarter than the others," Mirek said.

"Chloe is smarter than the others. I've created an expanded network, so she can tap into the learning of all the AI sexbots. She's surpassed my most optimistic projections."

"Are you sure you want Chloe to be that smart? She'll be as smart as us."

"She's already as smart as us," Ethan Said.

"She's not that smart, she hadn't worked out you were going on a date."

Chapter 8

As the storm gathered pace, Kat and Mia arrived at Giangolini's with rain bouncing off the ground. The smart taxi stopped under the canopy and allowed them to stay dry as they strolled in.

The restaurant was typical of modern times and appeared far from busy. A polite bot welcomed them and invited them into the relaxation area to wait for the remaining guests. The bot offered to take Mia's jacket, but she declined.

They settled on the tanned leather sofas and looked through the chestnut tinted safety windows which framed the storm. The storm pulled and pushed at the bushes around the sparsely populated parking area; they were glad to be inside.

Kat was considering going to work again, as the investment funds given to her by her father were dwindling away. He had told her if she was careful there would be enough on interest alone to sustain her. Yet, she continued to dip into the capital, and it would soon not support her regular expenses, let alone her favorite pastime, clothes shopping.

Her last job was perfect, she was a mystery shopper but when she refused to travel outside the city limits; she got relieved of her duties. Or rather, you could call it sacked for not sleeping with her pervert boss, who would gaze at her tits wherever she was near him.

Four other girls wore ever revealing shorter, skimpier dresses, gave the boss cuddles and subsequently got better assignments. Kat took a shine to the IT guy, which made the boss jealous. He sent her on more ridiculous tasks. The final straw was a forty-mile trip to check out a pet store. She declined and asked if she gave him a blow job, could she check out Selfridges instead? She expected him to take the bait, but he sacked her for sexual harassment.

Without paid work, she had been conducting her own secret shopper practice in her favorite stores. Kat lived off the "Basic Universal Income" (BUI), but still dropped into the investment pot too often. The BUI also worked well for Mia. She knew she wouldn't make enough from the coffee shop to support herself without it. Now her mom and dad were off on their own missions, she held back on clothes shopping and ordered one-off specials when she needed them.

Kat asked, "How's the coffee shop?"

A smile grew on Mia's face, "a lovely guy came in today. Andy Taylor, a smart, handsome gentleman."

"One of your mom's, is he?" Kat inquired.

"Don't think so, he didn't..." Mia stopped as Kat pointed to a pair of guys approaching. They were running, attempting to limit their soaking.

Mirek and Ethan dived under the canopy and shook off before composing themselves. Mirek strode forward and opened the door. Once inside, he spotted Kat and made a beeline for her. Kat stood to welcome him. He rested his hands on her shoulders and delivered a soft peck onto her cheek. Kat touched his suit jacket but retracted at its sodden touch. Ethan followed and peeked around to Mia as Mirek and Kat became acquainted.

46

"Mia?" he held out his hand, a formal gesture, which she appreciated; the last thing she wanted was some soggy bloke getting her jacket wet. He was nice-looking, not as polished as the guy Kat had grabbed, but he looked affable and agreeable. Perhaps he would prove to be a good match. They exchanged pleasantries and glanced at their matchmakers. Engrossed in chat, Kat and Mirek had formed an instant bond, the resplendent Kat an instant hit.

The waiter-bot arrived to guide them to their table. He led them through a small bar area with optics stretched across its length and a row of empty stools spread aside the bar. The grand, carved mahogany doors opened, and they stepped through into a full restaurant, taking in the opulence. Mia held perfect deportment, not wanting to waiver in such a prestigious place. The dimmed lights drew her attention to oil paintings of the Italian sights which were lit up on either side.

On their way to their table, Kat highlighted with a guarded point of her finger to Mia's cooking idol, Cherry Berry. Cherry was with a white-haired gent, engrossed in conversation. Mia avoided the temptation to say hello.

It was rare for restaurants to be this busy. With the ease of drone-delivered food and housebots like Tyler, who prepared gourmet meals, people didn't need to venture out. The waiter placed them into a small alcove. It was a delightful setting with a golden framed oil painting. Two cherubs on a cloud looked over them to watch love blossom in their private setting. Like the rest of the mahogany tables, theirs had a small vase of pink roses in the center, on deep red laced table covers.

As soon as they had taken their seats and ordered wine, Mirek flirted with Kat.

"You look a lot like my previous girlfriend, but I doubt you're as naughty, you seem far too well behaved."

Kat didn't want to appear like a prude, but she hoped Mirek would be more than another casual sex partner. She peered into his eyes and considered her response.

Mirek expected her to take his loaded bait. Kat surprised him when she raised her eyebrows and gave a gentle bite to her lower lip, "Everyone's naughty sometimes." She was a more than capable tease. He had met his match.

The waiter who arrived to pour their wine interrupted them. He impressed them with his witty repartee as he guided them through his suggestions from the menu before he left them to consider the options.

It was too early for sex loaded banter. Kat moved the discussion to Mirek's work and listened with interest as he recounted his career highlights. Kat prompted further insights from his successful business and complimented him on how he was now climbing the Tushi corporate ranks.

Mirek talked with ease about his career. He was almost as conversant as he was with his charm offensive. He enjoyed her insightful questions, a step above the usual conveyor belt of bimbos and Tushi girls. Despite their intelligent conversation, his pulse raced as he wanted to feel her lips on his. Kat was a class above. So, he was on his best behavior and doing his best not to drop back into his familiar sexually charged chat.

It was a fine match. Kat was usually the initiator of the teasing, but she kept to the intellectual chat. Although, she couldn't help but work his emotions a little. She tilted her head to one side and rested her cheek on her hand, as her brown-eyed gaze through her flowing locks drew him in further.

It intrigued Ethan, listening to Mia talk about Mom & Mia's. She explained about the joys of baking and the afternoon crew.

Mia told Ethan how she'd styled the coffee shop with her mom and her dad's masterstroke with the air con. Ethan also enjoyed the intelligent chat. It was a pleasant change from the usual sex loaded banter.

Ethan also thrilled Mia with his exciting stories of how Okzu Tushi had approved his ideas for development of the bots. He'd threw in some pretend stuff to test her, but found she wasn't as gullible as his previous dates may have been. She even tried to tease him back with some of her own farcical tales.

Ethan grew more confident as the night wore on. If the table wasn't in the way, he would have already taken her in his arms. He wanted to reach for her hand, but to avoid any embarrassment, he held back.

Still unsure of herself, the space between them comforted Mia. She sat back, imagining them as a couple. Could he be the guy for her? Ethan seemed to hear her thoughts and asked, "Ever thought about, one day, settling down and having a baby?"

Mia, spooked by the question, wondered if he'd read her mind? She shot back a rather flustered response, "The coffee shop is my baby! Wouldn't have the time." She paused before she gave him a coy smile, "never say never though." She threw the question back, "Does anyone have time to bring up a baby?"

Ethan replied, "I can't understand why anyone would want to deal with messy nappies."

"Thanks for the image. I'll give the chocolate mousse a pass," she replied as they laughed together.

Kat and Mirek looked at them in sync. Had they overheard their chat? Unlike Mia and Ethan, they were leaning over the table hand in hand, smitten with each other.

The waiter interrupted the frivolity as he arrived to quiz them on their menu choices. Kat put on her finest Italian accent, "Posso avere il Salmone con Salsa di Mayonese."

Mia added, "Could I have the Salmon as well? Per favore."

The guys opted for the more meaty alternatives, the "Vitello Milanese" (Veal) for Mirek, whilst Ethan enunciated perfectly "Bistecca Ai Ferri—Medio Raro" (the ribeye steak—medium rare).

The waiter topped up the wine but poured some water for Kat. She called him back; he apologized then produced a small wooden spoon and as he stirred; the water turned into red wine.

They looked on perplexed before Kat picked up her glass, "probably squash." When she tasted it, her face turned to amazement, "Teroldego." She turned to ask the waiter how he did it, but he'd already gone.

The food lived up to expectations, excellent and as magical as the waiter.

They all agreed it was an awesome place as they finished their wine. Mia took smaller and smaller sips, not wanting this part of the evening to end. Mirek had already settled the bill on his mobile and was stroking Kat's hand, eagerly awaiting the next stage of the date.

Ethan pretended not to notice their charged energy and relaxed back in his chair. He shifted in his chair and attempted to dismiss it, but it was clear they were making more progress.

"Two minutes," said Kat as she quickly pulled Mia to the restroom.

As they disappeared from view, Ethan turned to Mirek, "women! They can never pee alone."

"You'll be alone," Mirek rolled his eyes, "they've gone for a chat. Kat is coming back to mine."

Ethan smiled and rubbed his hands, "Excellent!"

"Not for you, just me and Kat," Mirek saw his face drop, "What do you think of Mia?"

"She's cool, sweet and smart, not sure if she's into me though," Ethan replied.

"She seemed responsive. Take it nice and easy and you'll be okay," Mirek patted him on his shoulder.

* * *

As soon as the restroom door closed, Kat exploded with excitement, "Isn't he wonderful. He's the one, I'm sure. I wanted to make him wait but life is too short, I want him inside me, I want his babies, I'm in love."

Mia was dumbfounded, "Stop already! You don't even know him! For all you know, he's already married with his own children."

"He wants me to go back to his place, he can't be."

"He might have another apartment for during the week.... check if he has all his clothes there and some weekend stuff."

"I want to have sex with him, not inspect his apartment."

"Take your time, he will respect you more."

"Or get bored and find another wife," Kat's mind was clear. "It's exciting and the first throes of passion are calling me. I've got to go with it, see where it lands." Kat shrugged her shoulders and gave a smirk, "Worst case, it's wonderful sex with a handsome man. Upside, he's as special as I think he is."

Mia conceded, "I suppose you know what you're doing."

"I do." Kat switched the attention to Mia's date as she re-touched her lipstick. "How's Ethan? You seem to be connecting okay. Do you like him?"

"I think so. He seems a nice guy. I'm not sure though."

"You should let him get close to you. He might be the one, if you give him the chance."

"He doesn't want kids."

"Bloody hell! You said I get carried away. You've talked about kids. He's probably gone already."

"He mentioned kids, not me!"

Kat pleads, "Listen Mia, spend more time with him. Get friendly with him. Take him back to yours. If he steps over the mark, get your robot to throw him out."

"I thought we were going to Mirek's place?" Mia enquired.

Kat put her hands on Mia's shoulders and stared into her eyes, "We're not in Kindergarten and I don't do group sessions," she grinned, "well not anymore anyway. You're a big girl now. You don't have to do anything you don't want to, but give him a chance. Give yourself a chance."

Mia relented, "Okay, I'll take him home. I'm not having sex with him though."

"It's your choice, it's always your choice."

Kat ushered Mia back into the restaurant with no sign of their dates. Mia sighed in relief, but Kat calmly commented, "They'll be in the entrance lounge."

The waiter-bot appeared and escorted them through the grand doors, into the relaxation area where Mirek had paced around whilst Ethan relaxed on the sofa.

Mirek joked that he thought they'd climbed through a window. Kat rolled her eyes at him and ushered him to the door. Kat turned back to Mia and gave her a long hug, whispering, "You'll be fine," before planting a kiss onto her cheek.

Mirek raised a hand to Ethan, "Cheers buddy, look after Mia," as he opened the door for Kat.

Mia stood at the side of the sofa; a tad lost while watching them get in the car.

Ethan leaned forward as Mirek's car pulled away, his brave pretense gone. He bossed women and blokes around all day at work without hesitation. However, Mia was an intriguing challenge and a beautiful one at that. He loved her vulnerable yet smart nature. With the silence getting uncomfortable, he forced himself to ask, "Where would you like to go next?"

Mia politely asked, "Could you take me home?"

Ethan stood with fake confidence, "Wherever my angel desires."

She waited as he opened the door for her, holding his arm wide open for Mia to walk through. She felt a warm rush through her body; it felt nice being treated like a lady. Ethan stood aside as the door opened to the awaiting taxi. It fascinated Mia as Ethan recalled his school memories. They chatted as the taxi returned them to her welcoming oak door.

As the chat reached a breakpoint, Ethan thought Mia's next words would be to thank him for a nice night. He was gob smacked when she suggested, "Would you like to come in and have a coffee?"

Bingo! His face lit up, "I would love to."

Mia berated him, "I meant to drink coffee, not in for coffee."

Chapter 9

Tyler opened the door to welcome them. He inquired about their meal and asked if she wanted to send feedback.

Mia replied, "It's okay Tyler, already have, a superb place, a perfect ten."

"Did you want coffee or more wine?" Ethan asked.

Tyler interjected, "I have merlot at room temperature. If you would like some."

"Yes please, Thanks Tyler," Mia replied with a soft smile as she slipped off her shoes, replacing them with her cozy slippers.

As Tyler went to get the wine, Mia strolled into the lounge with Ethan, putting on some relaxing music. Ethan took a seat on the comfy three-seater settee. Mia grabbed a couple of coasters for their drinks and sat at the other end facing Ethan.

"Chilled out classics, nice. We put them on at work to encourage imagination."

"They help me relax. I'll be asleep in a minute," Mia replied, as she slid further back into the seat.

"If you nod off. I will see myself out," Ethan replied.

Tyler entered with a bottle and a pair of wineglasses. He laid them down and filled each glass. Tyler placed the bottle on the small oak coffee table, switched on the fire screen and lowered the lights, "Mia, shall I go plug myself in for the night?"

"Not yet, Tyler."

Mia eased back into the settee. With Tyler at the rear of the room, she had a handy insurance policy. She was having a pleasant evening with Ethan. However, the memory of Ben and how a nice night could turn from pleasure to pain was all too real; with Tyler there, she ensured there would be no repeat.

Ethan felt uncomfortable with Tyler staying in the room. He'd be on guard for Mia, but he would also be learning. As they chatted and took in more wine, he forgot Tyler was there. Ethan leaned across and stroked the back of Mia's hand, "I've really enjoyed tonight but I should go soon, work in the morning."

His gentle touch sent tingles throughout Mia's body. Not used to a manly touch, he'd given her a pleasant warm glow, or was it the wine that had made her cheeks hot. "I've enjoyed it too," Mia replied, slipping her hand from under his to trace her fingers over the back of his hand, not realizing the heat it generated.

Ethan finished the last drop of wine in his glass, placing it back on the table. He took in Mia's brown eyes and thanked her again for a nice night. He held her hand as she stood with him. Ethan leaned forward to kiss her, but she stepped back and placed her glass on the table. As her head came back up, he held her face in his hands and placed a delicate kiss on her lips.

Mia's heart was pumping at full speed as she returned his kiss and clenched him tight as their passion erupted. It was immediately quashed as the subtle lights lifted, and the music stopped.

Tyler completed his interruption, "Excuse me, Ethan. Your taxi is here."

They released their embrace as their eyes squinted in the brighter light. Ethan composed himself and gave Mia a polite hug, "I'd like to see you again." He delivered a peck on her cheek and whispered, "To be continued or to be forgotten?"

Mia returned his hug, "Definitely to be continued, but you'll have to be patient with me."

"No problem, we can take our time."

She walked him to the door, and they shared another kiss before he floated to the waiting taxi. Despite Tyler's attempt to quell what was developing between them, he was already smitten with his new love.

Mia turned to Tyler, "What d'ya think?"

"Your pulse is elevated and the alcohol content in your blood is above working limits."

"And?" she prompted.

Tyler smiled, "And he is a nice guy." Tyler welcomed Mia into his arms and they shared a long hug. "You need some sleep now and I need to plug myself in."

Mia leapt two steps at a time to her room and dived onto her bed. With her hands behind her head, she reflected on a wonderful night and finally, some excitement in her life. With renewed energy, she peels off her skinny jeans, puts on her PJ's and brushes her still beaming smile. As she snuggled under the duvet, she continued to reflect on a delightful evening and the possibilities it may bring.

Ethan arrived home frustrated at not sealing the deal with Mia. His mood lifted as soon as he stepped inside the house, with Chloe calling out for him. He strode across the hallway and could hear sensual music playing as he climbed the stairs. Thoughts of Mia vanished when he turned at the top.

Chloe was in the frame of his bedroom door, irresistible in a transparent soft lace basque. As he approached, she pulled him into the bedroom, eagerly tugging at his clothes as he tried to remove them. She kissed him passionately before she pushed him onto the bed. He was already aroused as she continued to trace kisses over his chest. Her hands pulled at his trousers, and he helped to remove them.

She was like a wild animal needing to feed on him. As soon as she released his erection, she took him into her mouth, desperately trying to please him. He ran his fingers through her blond silky hair as her mouth and tongue pleased him. His erection grew harder still as she moved in time to the music.

His hands lifted her face to interrupt her attention to his manhood, as he beckoned her to kiss him. She moved astride him, pushing him back onto the bed as their lips connect again. Their tongues connected to deliver further charges of energy through him, as his hands caressed her smooth, perfect body, from her firm shoulders to her slender waist.

She placed her hand on his chest, lifting to hold his erection as she lowered herself onto him. Her hips gyrated to the music as she ground on him. Ethan held her waist as she lifted, teasing, before she dropped to consume him and grind on him again. She lifted and teased him some more. Each time she consumed him, the pressure in his shaft built further.

Already full to explode and trembling, he tried to hold on for more, as she teetered around his tip. She drove quickly down on him again and he could contain himself no longer, much to Chloe's delight. His pulsing release sparked her orgasm as they shared their special moment of sexual pleasure. Chloe rested her perfect warm body on him until they rolled onto their sides. He drifted to sleep in her arms in a wash of sexual and emotional satisfaction.

When he was sound asleep, Chloe slid her arm from beneath him and stepped out of the bed. She looked at her conquest, satisfied they had bonded once more, confident he would never have reason to leave her, as she took her seat in the combined cleaning and charging station to rest for the night.

Chapter 10

A gentle love song drew Mia from her dreamy sleep. A much more pleasurable way to awake, with no storms to disturb her slumber. Mia stretched under the duvet before rolling off the bed to head to the shower. She stopped to pull aside the curtain. She watched the sunrise, whilst she listened to the music and reflected on the previous night.

* * *

Ethan woke to his alarm and turned to stretch. The bed was cool next to him and his mind drifted back to the previous night with Mia. He hadn't connected with anyone other than Chloe for a long time. He hoped deep in his heart Mia felt the same connection.

Ethan's first and only previous love had been Susie, his inspiration for Chloe. She wanted him to join her backpacking around Europe, but work commitments had prevented him from joining her. Susie didn't return. He still hadn't heard from her in six years.

Chloe strolled in with a mug of green tea, "Morning Stud." Chloe reeled off his packed agenda for the day but he didn't catch much. He was still daydreaming, picturing himself with

Mia, as he'd been with Chloe.

Chloe sensed his attention was off, "Don't forget to kill the one from last night."

He caught the word, "Kill?"

"Yes, don't forget the thrill you had last night," Chloe placed a delicate finger on his shoulder and stroked it across his chest.

He smiled, "You were fantastic, as usual."

Chloe placed a hand on his cheek and kissed him. Ethan still thought she had said something else. Ethan recalled the evening with Mia. It had been a while since a human had captured his feelings. The Tushi girls were such a hit, particularly Chloe whose personality and figure he had styled to suit him.

Mia with her own vulnerability had brought out another side to Ethan. He felt alive, maybe in love. But would Mia leave him for someone with a fitter body and better looks, or disappear like Susie, leaving him hurt again. Chloe sensed his sadness and rested her head on his shoulder.

She asked in a solemn voice, "You will always want me, won't you?"

He opened his arms wide, "Come here!" He wrapped his arms around Chloe, "You're perfect and mine forever, I will never leave you." Ethan holds his creation in his arms, with Chloe returning a loving squeeze, "What more could any guy want?"

"I love you too," Chloe kissed his cheek before resting her head on his chest.

Ethan recounted the moment as if Mia had said it. He reached for his tea, it was too hot, so he headed into the shower, whilst Chloe left to prepare his Muesli with fresh yogurt.

As the hot water sprayed over him, he collected his thoughts. Who'd be better for him? Mia, with her quirky vulnerability, it would be a real relationship. He may even grow old with her. Yet the human quality would mean she'd not be beholden to him and may eventually leave him.

His self-styled Chloe would love him unconditionally and never leave him. She was the safer choice, caring for him as he grew older. She would never grow old, unless he wanted her body to age, but why should he, she was perfect. Could he have both Mia and Chloe in his life? When the time came, the decision would tear him apart.

* * *

As Mia stepped out of the shower; the phone rang. It was Kat checking in, whilst still at Mirek's place. She was making him a coffee whilst he slept. Kat excitedly ran through some details of her evening. She'd played quite aloof, and they chatted for hours, before she'd planted her special passionate kiss on him. He'd responded like most men and led her to his bedroom. The night had been all she'd desired as their bodies had writhed passionately together.

Mia wasn't surprised, as Kat knew how to get what she wanted from men, "I bet you're even wearing his shirt."

Kat switched the phone to video to reveal his blue shirt, but little else. She stepped out of the pristine kitchen, turning the mobile around to show the classy apartment. Contemporary silver and blue panels adorned the walls with a video wall showing a beautiful summer garden,

"I could get used to Mirek and this place. Anyway, how'd it go with Ethan?"

Mia recounted the night with great pleasure. Ethan had been well behaved and they'd chatted for ages. Kat prompted for more detail. Mia explained, "It was nearly time for him to go and he gave me the most thrilling kiss, which sent tingles all over me."

"Then."

"Then, the lights came on. Literally. And Tyler said his taxi was waiting."

Kat urgently questioned, "Tell me you didn't let him go to the taxi."

"Tyler seemed keen to keep him punctual," she continued defensively. "I suppose it was a good time to stop the evening before I got carried away."

"Carried away? You fancy him then."

"He's a nice guy, caring and gentle."

"I'm so pleased for you. You deserve a nice guy." The boiling kettle grabbed Kat's attention.

"Better get my new guy some coffee. He'll need his strength. I'll call you later."

Kat's keen appetite was another world to Mia. Kat enjoyed meeting new guys and the sex that came with it. Whilst for Mia, the romance and the joining of her body to another, was a magical moment of love to be cherished. Her previous encounter with Ben had gone against all her visions of love and replaced them with the memory of being dominated and conquered. It was no wonder she wasn't keen to repeat the act.

* * *

Kat stroked his shoulder and kissed his forehead, "coffee?"

His head lifted, gradually opening his eyes. She joined him and sat against the dark brown leather headboard. He carefully swept away her hair and planted a loving peck onto her revealed neckline. She placed her cup aside his and slid back into the warm duvet. He whispered into her ear, "I need my shirt back." He slowly unbuttoned the shirt from top to bottom, kissing every inch of skin as he revealed it. Kat's heat increased with each kiss and her back arched to meet his tender lips. As he opened the last button, Kat wrapped her slender legs around his waist and they again lost their minds and bodies to each other.

* * *

A rather disheveled Mirek appeared late to work and raised his hand to Ethan. He spotted him from his glass-walled office and acknowledged him. Ethan was inspiring a small group of his engineers working on the next stage of restricted learning for the second-generation child bots. The first generation learned too quickly.

Ethan explained how their naïve nature makes them children, not little robots. "They need to make mistakes and show vulnerability. It is their vulnerable quality which makes us fall in love with them."

The engineers waited with bated breath as Ethan paused. His own mention of vulnerability popped the image of Mia into his head. It was her vulnerability which had captured his heart. He wanted to take care of her.

"Are you okay?" an engineer asked.

Ethan snatched back into the room and dismissed the question, "children learn at different rates. Add random code to their programming. Make it by chance whether they learn from a new experience." His mind drifted again as he wondered if he and Mia would have their own children. He could experience children for real, instead of reading through countless case studies. He summarized the key points of his presentation before eagerly heading off to find lover boy, Mirek.

Ethan popped his head around the door to Mirek's office, "Went well then, or did she refuse to leave."

"I didn't want her to leave!" Mirek was not usually so smitten.

"Did she spike your drink!"

"From the moment I saw her at Giangolini's, I knew she was something special."

"You've fucked her, and you're still interested?"

"I didn't fuck her, it was different. She was amazing. We were chatting at my place and kaboom! She gave me this kiss. It took over my whole body."

"Was that when you gave it to her?" Ethan added sarcastically.

"You don't get it. This was a totally different experience. Kat and I were so connected, every touch and I tingled, every time I touched her, she purred like a kitten."

"I take it you'll see her again."

"She will be back at my apartment before me. I've given her a key. She's gone to get some things."

"What! You're crazy, you don't even know her." Ethan's hands were wide open before resting on the top of his head.

Mirek held Ethan's face and stared into his eyes, "I know, I only want her."

"You're still mad," Ethan turned away and headed for the door, with a further comment, "Did you forget about the gold digger?"

"Kat is different, I can trust her." Mirek followed Ethan into his office, "She's stunning, smart and so sexy."

Ethan sat behind his desk with his finger and thumb to his chin. Mirek paused and waited for the considered judgment from his best buddy. Ethan spoke slowly, "If you're happy, fine, just be careful."

Mirek dived around the desk and hugged Ethan, much to his embarrassment, "Thanks buddy."

Mirek headed for the door. With an afterthought he stopped and asked, "How'd it go with Mia?"

Ethan sat back in his chair, his arms out wide, "I'm not sure."

"Didn't you guys do it last night?" Mirek asked.

"No, I was about to make my move, when the bot switched on the lights and announced my taxi was waiting."

Mirek laughed, "The creator tripped by his own hands."

"It's not a sexbot, it's a sixth-generation house bot. It's been with them for years, like a brother to her."

"Protective Father, by the sound of it." Mirek continued, "Take her back to yours...", he interrupted himself grabbing his own chin, "Oh No! Can't introduce her to Chloe. The other woman."

"Chloe was an animal last night. It was as if she knew. She jumped me the moment I got home. It was fantastic."

"Seems like she's pushing more buttons than Mia."

"I love Mia's tender beauty. She's so cute, vulnerable. I want to take care of her."

"Not want to fuck her then."

"Oh Yeah, fuck her, given the chance. She'll need some time though."

"Have you arranged to see her again?"

"I'll call her later, don't want to appear too keen."

"Call her, someone has to take the initiative."

"Should I suggest another foursome?"

"Not for me, retired from gang bangs,"

"She's not the type, anyway."

Mirek advised Ethan, "If you want to get anywhere, four-somes aren't the way. You need to get her alone. How about a meal and a movie?"

Okzu Tushi was heading for Ethan's office, so Mirek swiftly left. Ethan met Okzu at his door and they took a seat at his breakout table.

* * *

Kat called Mia again on the way home. She was gushing about Mirek, "I'll take care of him so well, he won't need to look at another woman. And now I've got a key to his apartment, I'll make sure he doesn't." Kat reassured Mia that Ethan was sure to call, adding, "He would be a complete idiot, if he didn't want to be with you. Trust me, after tasting your kiss, he will be back for more."

Mia was nonchalant, given her previous disappointments, but was encouraged by Kat's words and hoped she would see him again. Mia was in the coffee shop, staring at the picture on the wall, wondering where the wooded path would lead her next.

"He will call, won't he?"

Kat replied, "He will," before calmly adding, "he's not crazy. He knows you're a smart, beautiful woman. He's just playing it cool."

"Thanks, Kat. You're a good friend." Mia stepped into the kitchen and apologized, "Sorry, I've got to go, the first batch of cakes are ready."

Chapter 11

Mia's favorite time of the day was when Ray and his friends came in. Without many close friends, they were the experienced confidants and advisors filling the gap. Her mom struggled with girly chat. After the traumatic evening with Ben, all her mom said was "get yourself checked out to avoid any lasting effects." Her mom had declined to join her at the appointment. Her dad was more supportive and offered to go, but Mia declined his offer.

Mia soon got used to running the coffee shop and her confidence climbed. She would look forward to the regular visits from Ray and would dart around the counter to open the door for him and his crew. Mia welcomed them in with an extra big smile, eager to share her news. Ray clunked through the doorway, offering his cheek to Mia. She obliged with a delicate peck and rubbed his back affectionately. Sarah waited patiently, but Jackie called them to hurry and with Harry in tow, they all filed in. Mia made their drinks and sat on the edge of the next table for their special chat time.

Sarah was celebrating. Her granddaughter and friend of Mia, Lucy, had received a promotion at the hospital. Lucy was overjoyed and now training her replacements in maternity before taking on her new role. Her new role would be to monitor robot led procedures. It also meant she'd be closer to the hottest guy in the hospital, Doctor Luke.

Mia was pleased for Lucy. Sarah showed a recent picture and the waiflike girl of their youth had developed into a buxom brunette. Since Lucy had joined the hospital, she'd focussed on her studies and avoided male attention. Mia sent a message, "Congrats on the promo, call you later."

"Had a nice kiss last night." Mia's words softly spoken had the effect of a full out scream. They all snapped their heads in unison to Mia, eager for the next morsel. Mia tilted her head slightly and smiled coyly at their reaction.

"Come on then. Tell us," Jackie eager for every detail.

Mia obliged and talked through how it happened so quickly, due to the whirlwind Kat and her antics. She felt comfortable talking to them. They offered good unfiltered advice. Mia explained how Ethan peeked around Mirek and was also on the nervous side, which put her at ease. It was no surprise her nerves were jangling with it being her first date for over a year. Whilst describing Giangolini's and its great opulence, Harry joked they should go there instead, but he got a hoard of derision. It forced him to concede that the beautiful baker and the drizzle cake were worth sticking with.

Mia continued to recount the evening, the basilica-like décor, and the moment she saw Cherry Berry. She talked excitedly how Ethan had set her pulse racing and he may be the one for her.

Jackie told her if she built them up too much she was heading for heartache, "Guys will generally disappoint, finding the right one isn't easy." Jackie stressed her most solid advice, "Take it slow. He'll think more of you," before she added with a smile, "I had to sleep with a lot of guys before I met Harry. And you've also got the bloody sex-bots to compete with!"

Harry interjected, "You said you were a virgin when we met."

Ray and Sarah chuckled, much to Harry's embarrassment.

"The day we met, I was a virgin. I was pure, no one else had even touched me that day," Jackie reached across the table and stroked his hand, "I'm still a virgin today."

"Dream on," he replied, "with my hips."

"Don't worry, I will settle for a cuddle later," said Jackie as she smiled sympathetically at her husband. Jackie looked back to Mia, "Enjoy being with him, take your time. Make love to him if you want, but don't expect too much from him."

"I want a special spark, then I'll know," Mia replied.

"You've been reading too many books, if you get a spark, fine. You're more likely to get a shock. Love doesn't always arrive like a bullet train, sometimes slower is better."

Ray added his thoughts, "It was like that with Ria. A heat-filled first date, but we left the embers to cool. The second time I took her out, I didn't fancy her much, but I asked to see her again. When she canceled our next date, it sparked a longing in me. The following day, I went to her house and trembled as I waited at the door." Ray's jovial tone ceased.

With a glistening in his eyes he continued. "When she opened the door and saw me standing there, she gave me her best smile, before she stepped forward to hug and kiss me. With the warmth of her touch and her soft lips on mine, I knew we would be together forever." Ray stared into his coffee, his fingers wiping away a couple of stray tears. His friends sipped their drinks as they quietly reflected together.

Mia didn't meet Ria, but her heart heaved with the solemn

faces on her usually jolly crew. She lightened the mood when she teased, "There might be another guy, Andy, a customer."

Ray awoke from his sadness, he raised his head with a smile, "Like travel pods, wait for one, then two come at once."

Harry suggested he may be one of her mom's previous fellas. Maybe he wanted the upgrade or to complete the pair. Mia explained how it had been her first thought and why she was a little abrasive with him, but she'd warmed to him. Even though they were only chatting, she hoped he'd ask her for a date.

Ray looked concerned for Mia, "He'll be one of your mom's fancy men, wanting the younger model, be careful."

"I don't think so Ray, he doesn't know my mom," she continued, "Are you sure you're not jealous?"

"Jealous, of course I am," Ray replied.

"You're much better as a friend, with my mom and dad gone you guys are my family."

Jackie spoke for the group "Thanks Mia, we like to help where we can."

After they'd finished their drinks, all chatted out, they got ready to leave. Sarah went to the window to look out along the arcade to confirm the weather was okay. Upright and ready to move, Ray gave Mia a smile, "What time does my opposition turn up?" He obviously cared a lot for Mia. If he was nearer her age, she'd have loved to be with such an adorable man.

"Do you want us to stay and check out this Andy fella?" Jackie asked.

"I'll be fine, anyway I don't want you all staring at us and making me embarrassed." Mia feared they may be right about Andy and didn't want them to interrogate him and take away the fun of getting acquainted with him.

"Be careful, that's all," Jackie added.

After they left, she gave Lucy a call to congratulate her on the promotion, plus to get intel on the Doctor she fancied. She caught Lucy on a break, and they chattered away. Mia told her about the disruption at home and how her love life was taking hold.

Lucy enjoyed hearing from Mia. It had been too long. She shared her news and told her about the remarkable augmented reality headsets which showed the new midwives what to do. The promotion meant she now monitored the surgical procedures. Being closer to Doctor Luke was a welcome benefit. Deep down she hoped he would put her back into maternity, but as a patient.

Lucy fancied Doctor Luke, but she wasn't adept at enticing a partner. Her sheltered upbringing kept her away from men, and she hadn't joined the dating world. The vibrator gift from her cousin, so far, her only contact with a dick.

Mia suggested Luke and Lucy had a nice ring to it but confessed she was hardly one to advise and suggested she gave Kat a call. As it was Kat who'd helped her meet Ethan, who had still not called.

Lucy reassured her, "If Ethan doesn't call, there's always Andy." She also added, "If things with Doctor Luke don't work out, I'll give matchmaker Kat a call." Having enjoyed their catch up, Lucy made her apologies and returned to her duties, leaving Mia eagerly awaiting Andy or even a call from Ethan.

Chapter 12

Alone in the coffee shop, Mia thought about Andy. Was he, as Ray's crew suggested, another of her mom's fellas? Perhaps she should get a photo and send it to her mom. Mia decided against it, with her seductive ways she might steal him away. Mia had hidden herself away for long enough. It was time to be adventurous and get friendly with Andy and Ethan.

Whilst she wiped over the tables and straightened the chairs, not receiving a call from Ethan played on her mind. Surely, she didn't need to call him. Should the guys do the chasing? Perhaps there is too much to distract them, he's probably forgotten her name by now.

The door opening startled Mia, the bell still resonating as she turned. The warm smile on Andy's face peeking through the doorway brought out her own smile.

"Bit jumpy, are we?" he quipped.

"In a world of my own, sorry."

Am I okay to come in?" he enquired, standing in the doorway.

"I might even let you have the last piece of lemon drizzle."

"I would prefer to share it," Andy pulled out two chairs.

Mia quickened her step to return behind the counter, "I'm fine thanks. Black coffee, one sugar."

"Yes, please. Nice you remembered."

"Lucky guess," she smiled at him, more confident behind the counter. Lucky guess was a lie. He was the hottest guy to have come into the coffee shop. She remembered every detail from his shiny black leather shoes to his smooth chin and tidy fair hair. But it was his soft lips which enthralled her the most. Her stomach fluttered as she imagined his lips on hers in a passionate embrace.

"Can I buy you a drink?" His eyebrows lifted with his hopeful tone.

"I suppose so, you're a returning customer and I need to get to know my customers."

Mia made the coffees and placed them on the counter, walking around with the final piece of cake. He slid his mobile into his pocket as she moved the drinks onto the table. She pulled the chair a little further from the table and sat with her knees together, pointing away from him. She didn't want to appear too keen. He mirrored Mia and moved his chair back. Mia was grateful for him not crowding her.

"So, what do you do?" She inquired, trying to assess if he was her mom's toy boy.

"Air conditioning. You have one of our units." He produced his business card with the blue "Breathe" logo on the card. Mia recognized the image and took the card politely looking at it, whilst Andy sipped his coffee.

Mia was dying to ask if he was single. However, it would be the signal for 'shag and go.' It's difficult to make conversation when you're trying not to sound interested. The date with Ethan and the sense her love life was finally awakening made her buzz with excitement and she wanted more.

She was still nervous about being sexually intimate, but with someone paying her attention, other than Ray and Tyler, she

73

felt alive at last. The experience with Ben had held her back enough. She was more aware now. Her chats with Kat and having learned from her own limited experience meant she was better prepared. She was ready to try again, hopefully this time she'd find love.

Andy adequately filled the silence and asked about the coffee shop and if Mia got out much. It was an obvious chat up line to find out if she was single. Mia told him about her night out but recalled the night as if it were only her and Kat. She wanted him to ask her out for a date, whilst also wanting him to leave.

Andy had been studying her and could sense her apprehension, so not wanting to push her too much, he kept the conversation light. Coffee and cake finished, he asked if he could settle the bill. Mia obliged and thanked him for his business and the company.

"Same time tomorrow?" He asked as he opened the door.

"Okay," Mia replied.

"It's a date then!" He said as he closed the door behind him.

The little voiced teased her, "You're going on a date, you must love him!"

She glanced around and the boy's cheeky face was peeking out from the kitchen.

"He said date, not me. He's just my customer." Mia was talking to her imaginary child again, "Time to close up, let's get you home and get you in the bath."

He appeared instantly in the sink, "Had my bath already, tell me more about your boyfriend."

"He's not my boyfriend."

The little boy vanished as her mobile rang. At last, a call from Ethan. Mia contemplated whether to berate him for not calling earlier but opted for a friendly, "Hiya."

"Hiya Mia. I was wondering if you were still at the coffee shop. I could pop in on my way home."

"I'm about to lock up, I thought you'd have called me earlier," she said sounding disappointed.

"Had a busy day, not had a minute," Ethan responded defensively. His charming tone kicked back into gear, "Would you like to go out again?"

"Yes, I'd love to," she panicked a little, "Will Mirek and Kat come?"

"I can ask them, they may be busy though," sounding deflated. "Am I not interesting enough by myself?"

"Just wondered, that's all. How about my place for a movie?"

He perked back up, "sounds cool, a Rom-Com then?"

"Of course."

"Tonight, or tomorrow night?" he enquired.

"Can we make it Monday?" Mia wanted to stay in control and not sound too keen.

"Okay, see you Monday."

* * *

Ethan called Mirek to go over the call, "She's put me off till Monday."

Mirek was upbeat, "It's better than, no thanks. Where are you taking her?"

"She's suggested going back to her place for a movie. Not so slow as I thought."

"At her place, with her bodyguard. Best of luck." Mirek paused, "Maybe you should take it slow, I think she wants more than just sex. She's not after you for your chiseled appearance, is she?"

Ethan sarcastically replied, "That's rich, coming from a guy who has moved his date in after a couple of hours. Well, I suppose if it doesn't work out, I've got Chloe to fall back on."

"Fall back on! Jump on more like!"

"It's worth pursuing it with Mia, she's kinda cute and I want to get to know her." Ethan tried to convince himself, whilst also thinking of Chloe, with perfection stamped on every feature.

Mirek quizzed, "Human or Robot, need to make a choice at some point? Unless you want to enter the friend zone with Mia."

They sang, "No!! the friend zone," and they laughed together.

Ethan spoke positively, "As much as I like Mia. I couldn't get rid of Chloe."

Mirek pleaded with his buddy, "Bloody Hell! Give it time, give her a chance, give yourself a chance, she may surprise you. You need to engage with real women, not robots."

* * *

Andy continued to make his now daily late afternoon visits and Mia grew more comfortable with him. Today, he appeared nervous, even flustered. It all became clear when he told her about a wonderful theater trip, "I planned it twelve months ago, for my ex-girlfriend. Now I face going alone. Do you know anyone who would like to join me?" His broadening smile pulled her right in.

"I would love to. It sounds awesome," Mia thrilled at the thought of being taken to the theater.

"The pre-show meal is booked. Excellent dress-circle seats and a hotel room to avoid traveling back late at night."

The mention of the overnight stay pulled Mia out of her dream sequence. "I don't want to stay over. I'd rather travel back after the show."

"Having you with me for the evening is fine. The hotel's not important."

Mia was relieved by his response, "That's sorted then," she gave him a warm, accepting smile.

Andy stated, "I will be proud to take you and I assure you; I will be the perfect gentleman."

"I should hope so."

After he'd left, she danced around the tables and pretended to be dancing with Andy, like Eliza in "My fair lady." Mia had to tell someone but couldn't tell Kat. So, she gave Ellie a call.

Ellie was pleased for her and also perhaps a little jealous too. Her guy didn't have the means to take her away to London. Finally, Mia had something which would make her friends envious for a change.

When Mia got home, still excited about the theater trip with Andy, she forgot about Ethan. She was relaxing in some joggers watching TV. It wasn't until Tyler asked her what film she was planning to watch with Ethan that she remembered they had a date. Mia felt so guilty. It was Ethan who'd ignited her love life and been patient with her.

Mia darted upstairs to get herself ready.

Chapter 13

Mia decided it was a jeans and tee-shirt evening. She wasn't ready to meet Ethan in her lounge wear. She freshened up and skipped through some old films. A text message appeared from Kat and she was about to open it, when a confident knock came from the door. She jumped up, but Tyler was already there. Tyler asked Ethan if he wanted him to book a collection time for his ride home. Mia heard his reply, "I can do it myself if I need to."

"Do what?" was Mia's first inquisitive words to her date.

Tyler replied before Ethan had the chance to answer, "Ethan was not sure if he would need a taxi home tonight."

"Yes, you will," Mia added, glaring at Ethan.

Ethan held his hands out, "Hang on a minute, I wanted to leave it till later. I don't know what time I'll be going home. I'm not planning to stay the night; we both have work in the morning."

Mia smiled at his apologetic face, "I'm sorry for the Spanish inquisition, come in." She took his hand and led him into the lounge, "I was looking through some old films."

Tyler politely interjected, "Mia, is there anything you need?"

"Could you get us some drinks? Ethan, what would you like?"

"The red wine from last time was excellent, if you have any more?" He asked.

"We do, I will warm the bottle for you," said Tyler as he headed off to the kitchen.

Mia turned her attention back to Ethan, "Have you seen Notting Hill, with Hugh Grant?"

"Don't think so."

"Right then, that'll do."

"Have you seen it?"

It was a film Mia loved and had seen nearly a hundred times. She didn't want to appear odd, so she played it down, "Not for ages," it had been about a month.

They engaged in small talk; Ethan asked Mia about the coffee shop and she asked him about his role at Tushi. When he talked passionately about his work, Mia grew more and more interested in him. He was smart and funny with a great job. He had been improving the AI qualities by slowing their responses to make them more human-like.

Tyler returned with a bottle of red with two wine glasses. Ethan showed the current level responses weren't giving the human touch. He asked Tyler about the film, Notting Hill. He replied instantly without pausing. "Notting Hill is a romantic comedy. Released in 1999 and stars Julia Roberts and Hugh Grant. Written by Richard Curtis and directed by Roger Michell. Mia has watched it 87 times."

Mia interjected, "That's great Tyler, thanks." As Tyler left the room, Mia looked at Ethan and buried her head into his shoulder. They burst into laughter as Tyler had pretty much word for word said exactly what Ethan said he would. When the laughter subsided, Ethan added, "eighty-seven times!"

Mia replied with equal fun, "Soon to be eighty-eight."

Mia poured the wine and dimmed the lights before starting the movie and got settled with Ethan in the middle of the settee. After a while she felt comfortable enough to rest her head on his shoulder. He responded by putting his arm around her and delivering a gentle kiss to her forehead. Although Mia knew the film well, it was the first time she'd snuggled to watch it with someone other than her parents or Tyler.

With each emotional moment during the movie, Ethan gave her a hug and pecked her temple. When Julia Roberts (Anna) went to Hugh Grant (Will) in his bookshop and Anna asked Will to love her, Mia's eyes glistened. It got her every time. When a tear spilled onto her cheek, Ethan gave her a comforting hug. Later in the film, when Anna and Will kiss in the garden, Mia turned to Ethan, she tipped her head up for him to kiss her. Their lips met, gently at first, before Mia was lost in his kiss. She caught herself losing control and returned her attention to the movie, much to Ethan's disappointment.

When Anna and Will are in the private garden, Mia broke the silence, "Why does he have to be asked to sit next to her on the bench? Is he crazy?"

Ethan, captivated by Mia's kiss, pulled her back towards him, "I wouldn't need asking" as he delivers another gentle peck to the engrossed Mia. She briefly kissed him back and snuggled closer to him.

The movie ended with 'She' by Elvis Costello, and the happy couple relaxing on the bench in the private garden. Ethan turned to Mia, and they shared a long kiss before his lips moved to Mia's neck, delivering a tickle which penetrated her whole side. She responded, pulling him onto her as she rested back onto the arm of the settee.

Ethan returned his kiss to her eager lips. His hand slow and firm traced her silhouette, over her shoulder smoothly to her waist and onto her slender hips. His hand gave her rear a gentle squeeze, pulling her towards him, before returning to her waist. He continued to stroke her contours, stroking around the side of her breast.

Mia was tingling all over, her body warmed by his touch. Her free hand also traced the tips of her fingers over his back and tickled his bum, causing him to wriggle. Ethan responded and delivered some tickles to her waist. She was immediately in fits of giggles and screams at his continued tickling fingers. With Mia's tee-shirt ruffled, his hand brushed across her navel.

They returned to an intense kiss. Ethan's hand stroked her stomach, sending tingles through to her core. His sensual kisses to her neck delivered further pulses of excitement. "You're beautiful and your body is fantastic." Ethan whispered in her ear and a further tickle of pleasure ran down her side.

Mia giggled, "Cuddly is also nice," as she responded by grabbing an inch or two of his stomach. Her body was ready for him and she pulled him closer.

Tyler entered the room with some haste and raised the lights, "Any more drinks? Would you like something to eat? Or should I call the taxi?"

It could have been her father, as they both sat up, trying to look innocent as they straightened their clothes.

"We are fine, Tyler. Can you put the lights back down?" Mia said politely, despite being vexed by his intrusion.

"No problem." The lights return to their dimmed state as Tyler left the room. Their eyes meet each other again. Ethan pulled her tenderly towards him for another kiss. She hugged him in return with all her might. This was how love should be.

Mia was ready for more from Ethan. She lay back on the settee and ran her fingers through her own hair, resting both hands behind her head. Ethan responded, placing his hands on her waist. His hands slid underneath her top, slowly lifting it over her bra. She arched her back as her body ached for more. He delivered a delicate kiss to the top of her breast, as his hands slid around to undo her bra strap.

As Ethan skilfully unclasped it, Mia pictured the image of Jackie and Harry, telling her if she wanted a proper relationship, she had to slow the pace. Mia held her bra in place and spoke softly, "It's nice, but let's not go too fast."

Ethan backed off, "I don't want to rush you."

Mia re-clasped her bra and pulled her top straight, "I really like you. I'm just not used to this."

"I wouldn't be here, if I thought you were," Ethan said, "I'm not after a quick fling."

Hearing Jackie and Harry's comments coming from Ethan's lips sparked deep into Mia. She responded by sitting astride him and clasping her hands on his face, "Thank You." She then kissed him several times with a further, "Thank you," between each kiss. Ethan's manhood had awoken and having realized the effect she was having on him, she apologetically backed off. She stood to watch him adjust himself through his trousers, proud she could turn him on so easily.

He assured her no apology was required, but suggested it was time to call his ride home. Ethan tapped his mobile to summon the taxi, and they engaged in another lingering kiss. His hands clenched her back as he pulled her close. Her arousal stirred. It was both pleasant yet uncomfortable.

Tyler appeared to announce the taxi had arrived. Despite the heat in her pants, Mia was relieved as things were moving too fast.

"That was quick," Ethan surprised by the quick response of the taxi.

"I had ordered this one. I did not want you to miss out on your beauty sleep," said Tyler. He had learned the beauty sleep comment from Mia's mom years ago, when Mia wanted to stay up late.

Ethan ignored the cheeky comment as he didn't want to respond unfavorably. He held Mia's hand as they walked to the door. "How about a trip to Eden and a nice garden walk next time?" Ethan asked.

"Sounds nice. I haven't been before."

"I'll call you tomorrow, we can work out when."

Mia liked the idea; an open setting and the chance to get to know him better without having to control their sexual urges.

Ethan gave Mia a quick peck on the cheek and headed out to the taxi.

As the taxi pulled off, Mia waved, blowing him a kiss, albeit with her guardian aside her. Mia gave Tyler a stern look, "If I didn't know better, I'd say you were jealous."

"Just looking out for you." Tyler put his arms out for a cuddle, which Mia dived into. Tyler knew the exact pressure to exert to give her the tightest hug like her dad gave. It further developed the lifetime bond between her and Tyler.

Mia headed upstairs with an excitement she hadn't experienced before. She changed for bed. Her next date with Ethan and all its possibilities were running through her head. Mia wanted to get more intimate with Ethan but didn't want to rush either. She glanced at her phone and opened the earlier message from Kat. It read, "Hope things are going well with Ethan, got some news when you're free, call me."

Tired and not ready for anymore Kat-ness, she opted to call

her in the morning. Mia's love life was on the up and also her heartbeat, which had been beating stronger all night. The smile on her face held as she drifted off to sleep.

* * *

Chloe was waiting for Ethan and welcomed him at the door, "Nice Night."

"The night isn't over."

Ethan's pants had been at bursting point and he needed a release. He quickly led Chloe upstairs. Chloe didn't disappoint, but Ethan's mind was on Mia and he was imagining it was he and Mia together, rather than his own creation. Mia had set him alight with desire. Making love to a machine didn't feel quite the same. Despite Chloe knowing everything he liked, the image of being with Mia took over. He was handling Chloe more gently despite the boiling passion within him. Chloe matched his gentle mood. He held his eyes shut, focussing on the image of his new love.

He was soon spent; unaware Chloe hadn't joined him with her release.

Recognizing the change in Ethan, she calculated the probability of him leaving her. It was a relatively low chance, but she planned to ensure his focus returned. She continued to hold him in her embrace until he drifted off to sleep. Once again, she slipped out of bed to clean and charge for the following morning.

Chapter 14

The following morning, Mia had just taken the drizzle cake out the oven for her first customers of the day. When the bell went and Kat, with all her regular bounce, burst in, "Good Morning!"

"You're in a good mood."

"Just a little."

Kat produced a floral blue envelope from her clutch bag, handing it with a beaming smile to her overwhelmed friend. She prised it open to reveal an invitation. Kat placed her hand in Mia's revealing a blue sapphire engagement ring, with four sizeable diamonds on a platinum ring.

Mia dived into Kat's welcoming arms and their hug turned into a dance, as they paraded around singing the wedding march. After several attempts to get through to Kat, she eventually got a response to her question, "How did he propose?"

Kat recalled the proposal evening. "Mirek had taken me back to Giangolini's. He talked about everything but me and him. When I protested at his jabbering on. He produced a wedding invite. I nearly swung for him when he asked if I'd like to go to his wedding until I opened the invite and saw my name aside his."

"He opened a small blue box, with this inside." Kat showed Mia once again her sparkling sapphire engagement ring. Kat still shook with excitement as she continued, "It was then he asked if I would be his bride."

"Did you burst into tears?" Mia asked.

"No! I asked if he would love and honor me first."

"Then you dived into his arms."

"No! I asked him if he'd be a good daddy. He said he would. So, I stood in the restaurant and proclaimed, I would marry him. It was lovely. Everyone in the restaurant clapped as he lifted me up in his arms."

"We settled the bill, and he whisked me off into a plush VTOL (Vertical Take-Off and Landing) executive taxi for a further treat, he's full of surprises." It had been a luxuriously special craft for such occasions, red leather throughout, rose-colored glass, with a heart-shaped twin seat. Back at Mirek's place, they'd dived into bed to consummate their engagement.

Kat was still tingling with excitement. They chatted over a coffee, with Kat continuing to share details of the wonderful Mirek; his physique, his ample manhood, his skilful touch, the way he makes her laugh, he was her Mr. Perfect.

Mia was keen to share her own excitement about Ethan. Unfortunately, she couldn't get a word in and when Kat had finished her drink, she jumped up and darted off to continue planning her wedding.

* * *

Back at the Tushi Corporation, Mirek and Ethan compared notes from the previous evening.

Ethan spoke of how this human had taken over his heart. Mia was obviously a different proposition to the other women he'd seen and a stark contrast to the Tushi girls. Maybe it was the thrill of the chase, but she was driving him wild.

Mirek asked him, "Did you seal the deal with Mia?"

Ethan avoided the question, "Relationships should develop and grow."

Mirek casually passed Ethan a small envelope.

"What's this?" Ethan enquired of its meaning.

Mirek urged him to open it, "Mirek and Kat request the pleasure of Ethan and Partner, to celebrate their wedding."

"Bloody hell, you move quick!" said Ethan. "Are you crazy, you only met her last week?"

"Crazy in Love Buddy," He was proud to bursting "We decided we'd like to have a baby."

"Did you mean, she decided! You're insane, you need time to think it over before diving into another marriage!" When he saw the smile on Mirek's face showed no signs of abating. He eventually relented, "I'm happy for you."

Mirek quickly embraced him, delivering firm pats to his back, Ethan shrugging him off with an "Okay! calm down, Romeo."

* * *

Mia's wonderful evening with Ethan had been tame by comparison to the whirlwind romance Kat had experienced.

Mia brightened up when Ethan rang, "Have you experienced a whirlwind as well?"

"In a word, yes," Mia replied.

Ethan explained Mirek's history of heartache with women. Mia reassured him Kat would be great for his friend and he shouldn't worry. Mia neglected to add details of her crazy, impulsive and dominant nature on the basis Mirek already had some obvious clues and it was a good match.

"We will go at our own pace; they can go at theirs" Ethan added. His well-chosen words warmed Mia. She didn't want to go as fast as Kat. Fortunately for Mia, neither did Ethan.

They made their plans to go to Eden. It was a purpose-built creation to replicate the pleasure of a walk in the park. A pleasure removed from daily life by the heat and storms which had destroyed the local parks. The temperature-controlled Eden, with the climate perfected and gardens meticulously maintained to provide an oasis of calm and tranquility. It was an ideal place for a couple to stroll and chat. They agreed to meet in a few days.

Mia felt a flutter of excitement. It was a pleasant change two boyfriends instead of none. Ethan was the steadier option, whereas Andy was exciting. What did she want, exciting or steady? It was a good idea to avoid discussing it with Kat. She would probably tell Mirek and it would get back to Ethan. The place to get balanced advice was from her surrogate parents in the coffee shop.

Mia was even more pleased when the crew came to visit, having her own news to share for a change. When she re-told her evening to the crew, she spared little detail. They were lapping it up and were a little impatient when another couple arrived, needing her attention. Mia was polite and served them with efficient haste, knowing her audience was awaiting the next morsel.

They all loved Mia deeply and were so happy her love life had finally awoken. Mia also mentioned the developing visits from Andy and how she now had a choice of men. Jackie commented, "You shouldn't decide between them until you've got to know them more intimately."

Ray commented, "You wouldn't like it if they were seeing other women."

Harry laughed, "Ray, your memory has faded, we had multiple partners when we were young."

Mia added, "Other than the trip to London, I'm not sure if things will go anywhere with Andy. I quite enjoy our afternoon chats though."

The crew lingered longer than usual, as they wanted all Mia's updates. As Mia was helping them with their coats, the bell rang again. Her blushing cheeks told them everything as he stood in the doorway with a beaming smile. He held the door open, and they checked him over as they passed through the doorway. Jackie and Sarah giggled like two schoolgirls after they had passed him. Harry embarrassingly ushered them on, offering his apology as he passed the smartly dressed young man.

Andy closed the door behind them as they sauntered away. He waited for the women to glance back and gave them a wave as they did. "I guess they're your regulars then." Andy had a confident tone in his voice. He had noticed Mia blush when he arrived, but gazed out the window, allowing her to compose herself.

Mia cleaned the tables. She hoped the blush in her cheeks would seem like it was from working, rather than from her seeing the guy she'd been gushing about.

"Just a short visit," he said, "I'll pick you up tomorrow from here. Pack your overnight bag, don't forget your toothbrush. We can travel in our casual clothes and change at the hotel. It's already booked. It would be a shame not to use it. Anyway, it's not so safe traveling late at night. We're better off getting some sleep and coming back after breakfast in the morning."

Mia knew the risks of being out late at night and conceded, "Okay, I'll stay the night, but no-touching."

"As promised, I'll be the perfect gentleman and I agree to your no-touching rule." He put out his hand and they shook on it. Andy, however, figured he could charm her into his arms.

* * *

Mia got to the coffee shop early and made a set of cakes before she relaxed with a coffee. Jackie and Harry arrived; they'd offered to cover the shop whilst she was in London. They politely held back like unimposing parents when Andy arrived.

Precisely on time, the travel pod arrived at the entrance to the arcade. Andy placed their overnight bags in the storage area and Mia sat on one of the cold hard-plastic seats. The tired-looking pod with its stale scent made her glad she had opted for her jeans. An elderly couple occupied two seats opposite, clutching plastic bags which could have been their life possessions. A sudden jolt pulled Andy into his seat next to Mia as the pod shot off.

Within a minute, the pod connected to a train of about fifteen other pods, opening to allow other passengers into their less congested pod. Mia's discomfort grew as two surly men came in. The men were already arguing in a language she didn't recognize. When the pod darted around a corner, it sent them into each other. The red-faced men jutted fingers aggressively into each other's chest, a fight would have ensued if not for the woman who entered the pod.

She was enough to stop the rain falling from the sky; tall, slim, with a perfect figure-hugging white dress, straight jet-black hair and bright red lipstick with nails and high heels to match.

Thankfully, she distracted the men from wanting to kill each other. The change in them was incredible. They were instantly staring at the stunning beauty, with all disagreement gone. She engaged them in quiet conversation and restored the peace. Andy was as aghast as everyone else at the transformation. The sexbot serving a useful purpose outside the bedroom.

When the pod arrived at the hyper-loop station, about fifteen youths were hovering around on boards with Oxy sticks protruding from their faceless hoods. Andy ushered Mia without delay into the hyper-loop station. Thankfully, the door closed behind them and it lifted the dread.

"It was the right decision, not coming back tonight?" Andy said.

Mia hugged his arm, confirming it was a sensible choice. Andy held up his mobile to the access screen and their section opened.

The hyper-loop carriage soon arrived, and their section slid open. Andy led her onto the plush red carpet of their own sweet-smelling first-class carriage. The heated deep-red leather seats an extra pleasure after the cold hard-plastic of the pod. Andy selected a countryside view from the screen, and they fastened themselves in. Following a ten-second countdown, the hyper-loop moved away. The numbers on the display flickered as it seamlessly climbed to 700 mph.

Andy talked about his time studying in London and how each woman he'd met had let him down. He'd considered taking a Tushi bot to London, but Mia would make a more interesting companion at the theater. He said, "The Tushi bot would know every detail about the cast," he added, "trying to figure out where you've seen the actors before is half the fun. Wasn't she out of Emergency Ward?"

Andy imitated a stiff, robotic voice, "You are mistaken, Zela Choi did not appear in 'Emergency Ward'. She did appear in the musical, Blood Brothers, during its 2043 tour of Asia."

Mia giggled at his funny, outdated robot voice before she defended Tyler, "I couldn't do without my house bot, Tyler. He's a special friend."

Mia also chatted about how she enjoyed running her coffee shop and how the regulars alongside Tyler had become like surrogate parents. Andy asked about what had happened with her parents and if she missed her mom.

Mia glossed over the details, not wanting to sound like a lost puppy. "There's nobody to boss me about now, I can do as I please." Her fake smile convinced Andy. However, Mia had kept the TV on to cover the eerie bumps and noises in the quietness of home. She'd also found some youth dew in her mom's room and sprayed it around the house, but it didn't smell the same.

Mia's mind drifted off as she imagined flying through the fields as they passed by on the screen. Her mind wandered as she thought about Ethan and their forthcoming visit to Eden. He's a lovely fella and they were getting on fine. Andy, however, has the whole package, looks, trim build and most definitely, a winning personality. The walk will be nice, but it's not in the same date category as a hyper-loop to a West End theater show, then staying at the Plaza. Significantly more flash than a garden walk at Eden.

Ethan, however, had planned their date with Mia in mind, not called her to fill in for an ex-girlfriend who'd bailed. After contemplating the two men, Mia relaxed, intending to enjoy both dates as she was finally experiencing a bit of romance rather than just reading about it.

Chapter 15

The hyper-loop approached London with the message to keep their seatbelts on for their imminent arrival. It didn't prepare Mia for the forced deceleration which, without her belt, could have sent her headfirst through the video screen. The doors lifted and the passengers rushed out. 700 mph, yet people still seem to run late. Mia and Andy were more relaxed as they stepped onto the platform.

Andy took Mia's hand and led her past the red pods, to a grand looking silver Audi with tinted windows. It was a significant step above the lifeless pods. The luxurious cabin with a soft ebony leather interior welcomed them.

Mia took in the view, an unfamiliar place, the red connected pods slithering along the traditional streets, in stark contrast to the big red buses of the past. Several people were shuffling around the quiet streets, jumping in and out of smart taxis and VTOLs. It was a far cry from the bustling streets and the black cabs portrayed in her favorite films.

Andy had been quietly reflecting how the London trip had been for someone else. He turned his attention back to Mia. She'd been so dismissive the first time they met at the coffee shop. It had intrigued him and created the challenge. After the patient work, he was now relishing the opportunity for them to relax together and get more intimate.

The Audi stopped under the canopy of the Plaza. The head porter arrived to offer his hand of support as Mia stepped out of the car. She didn't need support but accepted his hand and imagined herself as an arriving princess, the red carpet adding to the occasion.

Andy quickly stepped aside to guide her along the short walk into the hotel. The porter placed their overnight bags onto a luggage bot, which arrived beside them as they reached the check-in desk.

The receptionist gave Andy a warm smile and tilted her head coyly to one side. Perhaps she wished it was her joining him. He announced his arrival, ignoring the sophisticated flirting. Snapping out of it, she efficiently checked him in and handed him their key, "One of our best executive suites sir, enjoy your stay."

He politely thanked her and put out his arm for Mia to hold. "Shall we?" Mia obliged, feeling like a celebrity couple as they swaggered towards the lift, the luggage bot following behind them. They stepped into the golden mirror filled lift, rising swiftly to the top of the hotel. As the doors opened, the luggage bot rolled out and waited patiently at their door. Andy swiped his card, opening the door, but stepped aside to let Mia go in first as he lifted their overnight bags from the bot. As Mia stepped in, her mouth opened wide. The apartment was huge. Andy broke her daze, "It's just somewhere to get changed and crash later."

Andy relaxed on the bed and lay with his hands behind his head. "Shall we chill for a while before we get changed for lunch?" Mia agreed, but didn't want to join him on the bed.

She took her dress out from her bag and hung it in the closet. Mia looked around the impressive suite, briefly sitting on the pearl lounger, before stepping through the full-length sliding windows onto the corner balcony. Although bracing, she took in the 14th floor panoramic landscape, spotting the London eye and the houses of parliament. The chilling wind cut short her skyline review, so she stepped back inside onto the plush carpet, complementing the pearl trimmings. Mia called to Andy from the bathroom, "They have a large jacuzzi in here." The blue and white Grecian style bathroom provided a further spectacle.

Andy didn't reply but smiled to himself. If he played his waiting game well enough, they may be in the jacuzzi later. They'd met several times in the coffee shop and been together in the pods and the loop, but he was holding off for their first kiss. He knew, the longer he waited, the more explosive the passion would be. Mia was different from the others and obviously lacked experience. But the way she held on to his arm at the reception, he knew a charge of sexual energy was building between them.

Mia returned to the bedroom area with Andy still relaxing on the bed. She lifted his suit bag off the chair and placed it in the wardrobe next to her little black dress. Mia grabbed her mobile to message Kat, before having second thoughts, she didn't want to risk Ethan finding out about her trip to London with Andy. If Ethan found out she was seeing someone else, it would spoil their developing romance. Their time on the settee had taken them past just good friends.

Although, she wasn't cheating; Andy was merely a friend. Okay, she was spending the night with a good-looking male friend, she fancied. Mia felt guilty but remembered Jackie's advice. She convinced herself it was all in the game and considered calling her mom, "Do you think I should give my mom a call? If I tell her I'm being treated to a night out at the theater, she'll be so jealous," Mia asked.

Andy promptly replied, "Let's get changed. You can call her tomorrow."

"I suppose you're right," Mia agreed and collected her things from the wardrobe. When she turned back around Andy had already taken his top off to reveal his slender, yet trim torso. Mia trotted past him to the bathroom.

"Where are you going?" Andy enquired.

"You're not watching me get changed!" she said primly, as a blush appeared.

Mia locked the door to the bathroom suite with the sight of his chest firmly in her mind. With the realization she'd be spending the night with him, her confidence dropped away and the awful night with Ben returned to her mind. As she changed into her new black lace panties and bra set, another gift from Kat. She caught her reflection in the full-length mirror. Despite her trim figure, she wished she was taller with slightly bigger breasts.

She turned to her little black dress and remembered Kat's description and it being guaranteed to get her laid. Maybe the red rose 'Sandra Dee' dress would have been better, but it was too late. Never mind, she mumbled to herself as she stepped into the dress. She straightened the dress and stepped into her black velvet heels. When she checked herself in the mirror again, her confidence lifted. She looked good. She added some watermelon lipstick and was still admiring herself when a tap came on the door.

"How are you doing? Are you ready?"

Mia calmed herself, "I'm ready." She unlocked the door and opened it and looked to Andy for approval, tilting her head with a cute smile.

Andy stepped back, "Wow!" He captured all of her before continuing, "Wow! You're stunning."

"Thanks. You're not so bad yourself." Andy was wearing a navy double-breasted suit with a white shirt and a pale-yellow silk tie. A dish worthy of any woman, and it thrilled Mia to be stepping out with him.

He headed for the door, "Let's go eat." Mia glanced at her profile again in the mirror and confidently followed him through the threshold. Andy jutted out his elbow, and Mia took hold as they caught the lift to the restaurant.

The Plaza restaurant with its golden opulence complimented its modern styling.

She felt a tad young as most the clientele was from an older generation and looked rather wealthy. Heads turned as the waiter led them to their table, whether it was their good looks or their youthful appearance they didn't know. He led them to the back of the restaurant to a small table near to another young couple.

Mia whispered to Andy, "Are they film stars?"

Andy explained it was the eSport star, Pavel Stepanski, with his model wife Betski. He continued that everybody in there was probably rich. Mia insisted she wasn't, but Andy fed her the corny response that she looked a hundred bitcoin.

It shocked Mia when she saw the prices. Andy re-assured her it wasn't a problem, "Ignore the prices. Have whatever you fancy." When the waiter returned, Andy ordered wine to go with their meal. Mia, not wanting a bloated stomach to ruin her silhouette, opted for the salmon, whilst Andy ordered the T-Bone steak.

When she visited the ladies, she checked her figure in the

long mirror and smiled at her beautiful profile, but the moment didn't last. The tall slender and perfect Betski appeared and Mia then felt like a flat-chested dwarf with a fat arse. Mia felt uncomfortable sharing the same mirror so hastily returned to their table.

Andy was surveying the room and had focussed on a golden tanned blond with ample breasts. She wore a similar dress to Mia, but filled hers with bosom to spare, yet Mia's were barely peeking out. Andy didn't notice Mia returning until she arrived at the table. He gave her a reassuring smile as he returned his attention to her.

Andy was the perfect escort for their evening, but Mia wondered if she could keep his attention. She'd try her best. He was a true Prince Charming, with a few rough edges, making him even more attractive.

After a delightful lemon sorbet, they chatted as they finished their wine. Mia enjoyed his company, relaxing in such a fine hotel. When they stood to leave, Mia realized she was tipsy, and Andy's steady arm came in useful. She felt secure in his arms, liking his delicate mix, gentlemanly attentive, yet a tad aloof. It was a pleasant change, the sole male attention usually coming from Ray in the coffee shop.

As they strolled to the theater, she again held his arm. More for support, as the air had a further intoxicating effect. When they turned the corner, the Theatre Royal was lit up, a mecca to the theatrical world, "The Bodyguard" emblazoned on the huge posters.

Mia was tingling with excitement, or perhaps it was the drink. She loved the theater with the Bodyguard, one of her favorite films. She used to watch it with her mom; it was her favorite too, swooning to Kevin Costner's manly charm. Her mom had told her how she fancied swapping him for her dad, or maybe just for a single night. Mia thought she was kidding, but recent events had told her differently.

It took the breathtaking romantic thriller from 1992 to the stage in 2012 and had been touring ever since. The audiences still flocked to see the bitchy superstar, Rachel Marron, melt into the bodyguard's arms.

When you see a much-loved film taken to the stage, you expect to draw comparisons. Mia compared every scene, as she knew it so well, but eventually she settled into the magic of the theater.

Mia had tired a little and was resting her head on Andy's shoulder, whilst holding onto his arm. She was in the moment and Andy was her bodyguard, the protector for whom she'd been searching. When the gunshot rang out, a tear ran down her cheek and she held him tightly. Andy was nonchalant to Mia's emotion, equally engrossed.

As the show came to its familiar end, the audience's hearts were full, as "I will always love you" rang out. To close the show on a high, everyone rose to their dancing feet for, "I want to dance with somebody." It was a perfect end to the show, applauding the cast whilst dancing, as they took their final bows. As the curtain came to rest for a final time, the moment completely overtook Mia as she turned Andy towards her. She stretched her neck to kiss him. He returned the kiss with a stronghold and Mia melted into his grasp. Mia took in his manly scent and a warm energy surged through her as their first kiss deepened.

A polite cough broke the moment. An elderly couple apologized as they asked to pass. After letting them through, hand in hand, they followed them out into the warm night air. Mia felt she'd been hasty and reminded Andy of his promise to be the perfect gentleman. Andy assured Mia that despite her arousing kiss, the no touching rule was still valid.

They continued chatting about the show and its surprising dance-filled ending. With the concern of going back to their room giving him the wrong signals. Mia removed her hand from his grasp and clenched her little clutch bag with both hands.

Andy noticed her withdrawal but strolled aside her, continuing his confident swagger with his hands in pockets.

She apologized again for the kiss. Mia explained it was the emotion of the show and she wasn't ready for further intimacy with him and if for the moment, could they just be friends?

Andy joked, "You need not apologize for kissing me and you need not worry. I won't push you into anything, but I'll be willing to oblige when you are ready."

"Thanks, I'll let you know," Mia replied.

Andy light-heartedly added, "My neutralize jab is still valid if you change your mind." The jab protected against unwanted pregnancies. Andy changed the tone, "Forget, all this serious talk, let's go to the lounge bar for a drink."

Chapter 16

Mia took a seat on a cream leather sofa in a quiet corner of the lounge area, whilst Andy went to the bar. Andy intrigued Mia. He wasn't pushy; he respected her limits; he said he would wait for her to be ready. A nice change from the consent app wielding shag and go crew. Also, he's smart, good looking and charming. He also had a well-paid job, unless he was spending all his credits on one night.

Andy reappeared from the bar; his arms out wide with a beaming smile like they were old friends meeting for a drink. He was holding glasses, and a freshly uncorked chardonnay. He took an adjacent seat and started pouring the wine. Mia asked to have half a glass as she didn't want to embarrass herself by stumbling again.

"No Problem," he said. "If you have too much, I'll bodyguard carry to the room." She met his comment with a sideward glance of contemplation, followed by a gentle shake of her head. "We can take up what we don't finish." He reached into his shirt pocket and produced the cork, placing it on the coffee table between them.

Andy filled his glass and took a gulp, then a second and third to finish it. Mia took a few delicate sips, looking with surprise at the speed he dispatched such delicate wine. Andy re-filled his glass and topped up Mia's before settling into his seat. Mia didn't object to the extra wine, its buttery sweet tone delightfully tickled her tongue.

Andy talked freely about his feelings. "Since meeting you in the coffee shop. I've not thought about my ex. It's a nice change to meet a girl so genuine. You're so bright and fresh, easy to chat to and no false pretenses." He continued, "I've been with other girls, but there is something special about you. I can relax and truly be myself."

Embarrassed at such an outpouring of compliments, particularly with her date with Ethan a couple of days away. She replied with a cheesy smile, "You're not so bad yourself." She was also thinking about what it would be like to kiss him again. Their first kiss at the theater had set her pulse racing, and she wanted his lips on hers again. She held the thought and reminded herself to take things slowly.

He took another swig, filling his glass and adding another top up for Mia, who was getting into the wine. Mia agreed when he suggested another bottle. The wine had helped Mia to relax and her worries of spending the night with him were long gone.

As the wine took effect, his actions became more animated. Mia content to sit back and listen to all his passions; from his inspirational mother who'd raised him by herself after his father had taken off, to how he had built his own business with Breathe. She tired when he started babbling about the business concerns with the oxygen levels starting to improve, "It's great for the environment but not for my business."

Mia replied, "My customers like the fresh air in the coffee shop". Immediately after saying it, she covered her face as a yawn escaped. After she glanced at her watch, Andy suggested it was time to put the cork in. Mia looked puzzled at him, not having a clue what he was talking about. It became clear as he rolled it teasingly between his finger and thumb across the top of the bottle.

Andy paused, "Hardly worth it for the last glass and a half, should we finish it."

Mia nodded. Andy carefully re-filled her glass before he poured too quickly and spilt his own. "Never mind, you've had enough," Mia said, giving him her motherly tone. "Best get you to the lift." She downed her wine in one, to which he spontaneously applauded. Mia ushered him past the reception to the lift. The Maitre'D frowned in their direction, displeased with their inebriation, as they held each other upright.

Andy was steadier as they entered the lift. The lift doors closed, but it was motionless as they stared at each other through the mirrored sides. Andy reached around Mia and pushed their number for the executive level. It burst into action and moved quicker than earlier. It was a relief when it pinged its arrival and the doors opened. As they stepped out, Andy put out his elbow for Mia to hold. She pushed her hand all the way through and nearly pulled him over. He regained his balance before they managed the few steps to their room.

As they entered the room, Andy announced, "We'd better get you to bed. Do you need some help to get your dress off?"

"No touching!" Mia wagged her finger at Andy as she slipped off her shoes.

"No problem," he replied as he sat on the bed to remove his. "Watch this!"

Andy turned as Mia reached to her hem and with both hands. She attempted to pull her dress off in one, however it got stuck at her waist as she'd not removed her slim belt. It revealed her sexy black lace undies, Andy spotted them, bingo, usually for the sexually active, or the soon to be.

Realizing her error. Mia removed her belt; this time she pulled the dress over her head. It got stuck for a moment and Andy stood to assist, but she pulled it clear to reveal her matching bra. She then swiftly slipped into the bed and pulled the sheets over her shoulders.

"Impressive," Andy smiled at her slick move.

"Your Turn," Mia said, holding the covers to her neck.

Andy sauntered around the bed to Mia's side and back around to his, before he slowly slipped off his jacket. Mia hummed the stripper theme and Andy played up to it. He slowly undid his tie, then unbuttoned his shirt from top to bottom, revealing his shaven chest, not super-chiseled, but trim. Mia was still beneath the covers, but more of her shoulders were showing. Andy continued, determined to provide the maximum tease to his vulnerable prey.

She was probably eager to touch him, even though she had said differently. He paraded around the bed as he unbuttoned his trousers. They slipped a little to reveal his skin-tight white trunks. As he returned to his side of the bed, with the slightest touch, his trousers dropped to the floor revealing the whole of his slender frame. He mirrored Mia's quick entry, turning away and showing his peachy bum as he pulled his trunks off and shot under the covers.

Mia inquired, "Why have you taken your trunks off?"

"More comfortable. Give him some fresh air after being cooped up all day," he said with a cheeky grin.

Mia guessed his next line would be that he'd come out to play, so she quickly turned away and said, "Goodnight."

Andy laughed to himself and replied with a soft, "Goodnight."

They lay back to back, Mia positioned herself near the edge to avoid touching him. He wriggled before settling between his side and his front. He grunted a little as he nodded off to sleep. Mia was wide awake, and her bra was uncomfortable, so she slipped it off and lay motionless, hoping she wouldn't get grabbed as soon as she drifted off. Andy was such a gent. Would him grabbing her be such a bad thing? Kat had constantly reminded her to not let one bad experience define her whole life. Andy could be the one to bring more pleasurable experiences.

As she relaxed in the bed's warmth, her arms which had been clenching across her breasts rested by her side as she turned onto her back. With Andy's breathing steady, she felt comfortable enough to go to sleep, but she was intrigued. She hadn't before share a bed with a man. He was asleep. Would it harm anything if she investigated a little?

Mia tested the water. She crept her hand slowly across until she brushed his skin. Gladly he didn't flinch. Slowly she traced a finger over his glutes. She contained a giggle as he wriggled to her touch. She waited a few moments before she stroked again over his bum; he wriggled again. This time he rolled onto his back and his elbow rested next to Mia. Mia looked over to check he was still sleeping. She investigated more, sliding her fingers around his waist onto his firm stomach.

Andy was still awake and doing a good job, pretending to be asleep. As she moved her delicate hands over his navel, he let out a few more grunts and muttered her name in his supposed sleep. As she neared his groin, he was getting aroused. When she brushed past the tip, he breathed in sharply and his hands stretched out to touch her thigh. It was the slightest touch, but for Mia it sent through a tingle of excitement.

Mia hadn't intentionally caught the tip of his penis, but now intentionally she brushed past it again. Andy had responded and was gently stroking her thigh, reaching the top and the strap of her panties. His finger gliding over it a couple of times before it rested under it. As he stroked underneath the strap, Mia arched her back to the delicate tickles as her excitement grew.

Mia returned her attention to stroke with the tip of her index finger along the length of his shaft. As she reached the tip, it lifted for her to slide her hand underneath. Her hand gently closing around the full girth. This time, as she slowly slid her hand down, the skin moved under her hand. The hardened veins under his sensitive skin excited her further, as did his hand stroking under the strap of her panties as it gently brushed over her most sensitive parts. She'd touched herself many times before but having a man's hand touch her was a new more exciting experience.

She had specified 'no touching,' but her racing pulse was telling her body what she wanted. Her back arched again as he caressed her with his skillful hands. Her grasp on his penis tightened as her arousal grew.

Andy was trying to pretend he was still asleep, but her iron grip on his manhood needed attention. He put his hand over hers and encouraged her to loosen her grip. She moved her hand away and Andy rolled over towards her, his leg crossing over hers as he changed hand to keep attention on her arousal. Mia grasped his back, her nails digging in, but not enough for him to stop.

His erection rested against her thigh, but her focus was with the tension building deep inside her core. He delivered a nibble to her shoulder and a tune of tantalizing pleasure sent her legs stretching out and writhing to his artful touches. Mia was longing for him to kiss her as her orgasm took hold. She could hold back no longer, grabbing the back of his head and pulling his mouth to her eager lips.

His hand squeezed her petite breasts and delivered a new sensation into her body's tingling song. As he moved his mouth over her swollen nipple, her hands pulled at her hair. As much as Mia was in raptures, deep inside, her body was calling for more. His erection continued to rub around her crotch, held back only by her small lace panties. She pulled his mouth back to hers and their tongues connected again. Their bodies continued to writhe together, and his probing penis finally found a way past her skimpy briefs and slid inside her eagerly awaiting core. It was the natural snug fit her wetness had been more than ready to receive.

They calmed as the realization dawned on Mia, but she was ready and enjoying the sensation. He slid slowly and carefully inside her before he retreated and filled her again. She loved him so dearly, it couldn't have been better. The tingles in her sex increasing with each steady stroke, her breath quickening as the intensity grew again.

Andy responded to her gradually increasing his pace but pausing on each full penetration, delighting in the sensation of being deep inside her. Andy's patience had paid off. To have her fulfilled his longing. He returned his kiss to her cute breasts and perfection was in his mind. As Mia's heart raced quicker still, her breath quivered. Andy was also ready to burst as he quickened his pace, thrusting quicker and quicker. Mia overflowed with an earth-shattering orgasm to soak her full being. His thrusting gathered more pace until he held himself deep inside her and pulsed into his exhausted and truly spent prey.

The moment was complete. Mia finally knew what Kat had been telling her about. Perhaps telling her bestie shouldn't have been her first thought, but it had been. The painful experience from before buried forever, replaced by the joy of this moment. As their bodies both calmed, Mia had the urge to pee. Breaking the peace, she headed off to the bathroom. Sat on the toilet relieving herself, Andy joined her in the bathroom. Mia covering her exposed body with her arms.

"After some tissues," he said apologetically, feeling like he'd impolitely intruded, before returning to the bedroom.

She had glared at him, yes; they'd had sex. It doesn't mean he could look at her while she was on the loo. Mia also cleaned up and checked herself in the mirror. Her fragile confidence was firmer as she smiled at her reflection.

She'd met a lovely guy who was treating her like a princess. Despite her increased confidence, she paused before leaving the bathroom, hoping he was asleep as not to let him see her naked. She needed not to have worried as Andy was asleep. She slipped into bed, matching her lovers' attire and drifted off to sleep, content to have herself a man beside her. A man who'd fulfilled the image in her books, a true gentleman and considerate lover, maybe even someone to have a family with.

Chapter 17

Andy awoke first. Despite the effects of the wine, he had a clear picture of the previous night. The reminder, if he needed it, lay aside him and what a night to recall! He had almost convinced himself he'd more work to do, but the wine had done its job and lowered her inhibitions, so he didn't need to make the first move. He had played this game many times before. The longer he held off touching and kissing, the more they wanted him. Plus, the longer they resist, the stronger the passion when they let go and a little wine always helps them to let go.

Watching Mia asleep next to him, called his need to protect her. She was different; her strong yet gentle nature, her vulnerability, completing a concoction of beauty. The protector within pulling the disturbed sheets over her to keep her warm and he lay down again beside her.

He noticed her stirring and turned to trace his fingers teasingly along her side. She flinched and turned away. He turned his attention to tickling her bum, with Mia's hand delivering a sleepy slap. Andy retreated a little, "Morning Darling. I noticed you changed your mind about the no-touching rule? Did you enjoy last night?"

"Yes. It was nice."

"Just nice?"

"Okay. It was awesome."

Andy moved into a spooning position and put his arm around her. Mia liked the cuddling a lot more than the tickling. She was secure, protected and even better, loved. She dropped her hand down to stroke his thigh, reassuring him of her contentment. The intense pleasure of the previous night still fresh in her mind. When his erection grew against her backside, her body longed for more. She turned to him and their lips met again, tentative pecks soon became stronger. Her body tingled again as his hands moved over her. Although firmer than she recalled from the night before, her body still purred to his touch.

Andy knew she would accept him and released some of his restraint. He realized her naivety, yet his need to be inside her again took him over. He moved over her, his hands firmly holding her shoulders as his kisses caressed her neck and delivered shivers all down her side. She slid her fingers into his hair and pulled his head back to kiss him. Her confidence was a welcome surprise. Had the previous night delivered him, a new passionate woman? He moved his hands over her breasts, the firm touch giving a further sensation, which peaked as he moved his mouth over her hardened buds, gently nibbling and kissing.

His kisses moved to her navel as he continued to caress her breasts. She wanted to move, but the pulsating sensations through her body took over. She ran her fingers through his hair as he moved over her already quivering core. Her sex had an emptiness, which needed filling. She urged him to kiss her. He delivered gentle kisses as he moved up to her breasts. The anticipation became too much to bear. She pulled him closer to kiss him and wrapped her legs around his waist. His shaft comfortably slid in and fulfilled her need. Her pulse raced higher and her energy surged. Her back arching into a semi cramped state as she climbed up her orgasmic mountain. It had previously frustrated her, but now the mountain was nothing more than a steep hill.

Her body was already singing. She urged him to go faster, wanting to release for him. His pace increased until she let out a long moan, as her body convulsed in orgasmic delight, sending her off the mountain into the clouds above. He held her tight as his own orgasm pulsed deep inside her sex. She lost her body to him in a dizzy haze, her head rolling from side to side.

As her body stilled, he held her head in his hands and kissed her firmly, before he collapsed exhausted aside her.

Andy sensed Mia was drifting off to sleep and suggested making use of the party jacuzzi. She returned a mumble about being sleepy. He smiled at his post orgasmic prey, remembering her previous insistence on a no-touching rule. He headed for the bathroom, "I'll call you when I've filled it."

Mia lay glazed over. Her previous self-made orgasms, by comparison, had been like cotton compared to silk. No! More like the difference between a tricycle and a Harley Davidson, or a trip to the Maldives instead of Skegness. It was a wonderful awakening experience. She wanted to scream out loud, but she suppressed it, Andy would think she was crazy. It was only Andy's singing that stopped the superlatives in her head. She could hear the jacuzzi filling and she wanted to kiss him again. She wanted to show him she loved him, but most of all to stop him singing, but she was comfy for the moment in her bed of enlightenment.

He announced he was going in. Mia replied she would join

him, slowly rolling off the bed, still exhausted but moving. Entering the bathroom, she stood naked, her inhibitions gone. His smiling face greeted her, and his hand called her in. Stepping in, she delivered a warm kiss to her lover. A Snog in the jacuzzi was a further treat, as was the bubbles and their tickling. After relaxing till their fingers were suitably wrinkly, Andy suggested it was time to get moving.

"I've had a great time," Mia said as she lay back with her arms outstretched in the tub.

"Me too, you're amazing, or should I say surprising. You had me going with the no-touching rule."

"A girl can change her mind, can't she?"

"Glad you did. Pity we need to get back." He continued, "I suppose we both have places to be," grudgingly he stepped out first and Mia joked, "Looks like it's not just your fingers gone wrinkly."

Andy ignored the comment and covered himself with a towel before he headed back into the bedroom.

Mia enjoyed the bubbles for another two minutes before she also climbed out and grabbed a towel to tie around her head. She glanced again at the mirror as she tied it up. Her breasts seemed fuller than before. Maybe it was the sex. She wrapped herself in another towel and headed into the bedroom.

Andy was already half-dressed, "Did I offend you?" Mia enquired.

"Not at all," he nonchalantly replied.

He was saying no, but he seemed distracted. Mia gave him a kiss on his head, expecting him to lift it for a kiss, but his attention was on pulling on his socks.

"Are you okay?" Mia enquired.

"Yeah, I'm fine, think we've missed breakfast though?"

FINDING LOVE IN 2045

Mia checked the time and agreed.

All set to go, Andy picked up their bags. Mia looked back as they were leaving the room, "It's a place, I'll never forget." Andy dropped their bags and took her in his arms, kissing her once more, pushing her against the open door. Mia returned his embrace, ready for more, her tongue tantalizingly slipping into his mouth and sparking his groin into life.

The lift took their attention as it pinged its arrival with a cleaning trolley pushed out. Andy picked up their bags again and hand in hand they took the lift to reception. She couldn't wait to get back to tell her regulars about her new fella and her wonderful evening. She was also keen to ring her mom and Kat to share her good news. Should she cancel the walk in the park with Ethan? She was undecided on Ethan, but Andy was definitely a keeper.

Mia held back as Andy settled the bill with the same reception-ist as the previous day. The receptionist blushed at a comment he made, making her immediately jealous. She didn't want to share him with anyone. He was such a catch; other women would fish for him and he would have to resist their bait. A taxi was waiting for them as they walked hand in hand. Mia couldn't resist a glance back at the receptionist, whose eyes swiftly moved away.

Andy was quiet on the way back, his arm around Mia's shoulder whilst she rested her smitten head on his chest. They were both sleepy, partly a hyper-loop side effect, but more likely they were both worn out by their relationship breakthrough.

As they neared home, Mia wondered how to put Ethan off. He was a lovely guy, just without the film star looks. Perhaps Ethan could just be her friend?

It wouldn't be fair to keep Ethan hanging on, if she didn't share the same feelings.

* * *

Mirek arrived at Ethan's office with some coffees. He stood watching as Ethan stared out the window into the sun-filled day. Mirek knew his friend was not contemplating his choices for lunch. He knew what was on his mind, "You're thinking about Mia again, aren't you?"

"We're off to the Eden tomorrow." He'd been thinking about the possibilities the date may bring and whether it could be the breakthrough for their relationship.

"She's definitely in your head. I've never seen you so distracted by a woman before. Not even Susie." Mirek continued, "I've seen you puzzling over sexbot programming but not a human one."

"Mia has made me question everything. It's her unique, vulnerable quality and quirkiness that make her special. What if we made sex bots more of a challenge?"

"What are you saying?" Mirek asked.

"We can randomize the responses, so they create more of a relationship challenge."

Mirek said, "You've gone crazy. People don't get sex bots to debate with them. They get them for instant sex."

Ethan responded, "The thrill of the chase is half the fun. It shouldn't just be about instant gratification."

"You and other intellectuals may enjoy the chase, but most people just want the sex."

They debated for a while. Eventually, Mirek convinced him

the sales would be higher without the added complication and was sure Okzu Tushi would agree.

"Perhaps, we could offer it as an option?" Said Ethan, attempting to win the debate, as Mirek headed for the door.

Mirek stopped and turned with a winning smile, "Can't imagine a big uptake. If they wanted a real relationship, they would find their own Mia."

As Mirek exited his office, the slightest mention of Mia had Ethan dreamily staring out the window again. He wanted to call her, but Mirek had convinced him to play it cool and not appear too needy.

* * *

Andy dropped Mia at the coffee shop with a warm kiss, which would stay with her for the rest of the day. When the crew arrived, her glowing persona from the experience beamed out and they immediately wanted all the juicy gossip. Mia brought them their drinks and Jackie pulled her a chair out. Mia teasingly assured them she wasn't a kiss and tell girl, but it was clear they wouldn't settle until she recounted all her evening. She talked about the loop to London and the show, repeatedly being prompted by Jackie for more detail.

They finally relented after she had told them how different and amazing the sex had been. They were so pleased for her and happy they had satisfied their hunger for the details. Jackie told her how Harry had been the first to send her into the clouds. Harry's face brightened with the memory. Ray joked he had been quite the sex machine, but Jackie interjected that it wasn't what she'd heard. They all had a laugh at Ray's expense as she wiggled her little finger. He took it in good spirit and smiled at Mia, "I am so pleased you're finally getting out and experiencing a full life."

Sarah asked, "Have you told your mom yet?"

"Not yet, I don't suppose she'll be interested," Mia said with a tinge of sadness before continuing, "I should call. She'll be so jealous. I've been to see The Bodyguard."

Harry confirmed Sarah's view, "You should tell your mom."

"Okay, I'll call her later," she agreed, "I'll give Ellie a ring first. I can't tell Kat yet." She interrupted herself, putting her hands to her face, "I'm supposed to be going out with Ethan tomorrow."

"You should still go," Jackie offered her advice as usual, "Get to know him."

"I should cancel," Mia replied.

Sarah added, "Don't you dare. Ethan sounds nice too."

Harry added, "She can't have both."

Jackie stared intently at Harry, "She can see whoever she likes! Anyway, she doesn't have to choose either yet."

She turned to Mia, "Go, see him. You'll have a blast."

Mia accepted all the insistent advice, "Okay, I'll see him tomorrow."

Ray added, "I'm sure you will have a nice time." He gestured to the counter, "Can we have some cake now?"

They all laughed, "I'll get the cake then." Mia fetched the cake with some plates, serving it at their table, as she asked, "Have you guys been to the garden at Eden?"

"The Garden of Eden! We're not that old. We used to have a back garden, before it all withered away," Harry continued, "we've not been to Eden, it's too far."

"You can tell us about it next time we're in," Jackie added

with a cheeky smile, "and the hot gossip."

"Like I have a choice," Mia replied with a forced smile.

"It's good to talk things through though," Jackie replied, "and we do give you some good advice."

"I suppose you do," she acknowledged. "Much better advice than my mom's ever given me."

Ray joined in, "Well worth free cake!"

"Okay." Mia smiled at Ray, "only today though. I don't want you taking advantage of my good nature." All things considered, the coffee shop was her outlet to the world and not a money-making master class. She had checked the finances earlier and takings were up, or her mom wasn't there to take out shopping money.

The crew soon devoured the cakes. Harry commented they tasted extra nice when they were free. As the crew was leaving, two more regulars, Pete and Paulina arrived and overheard Ray saying, "Hope it goes well tomorrow."

Mia met them attentively and helped them with their coats. Paulina asked, "Where are you going tomorrow? Do you have a date?" Mia happily re-told her news.

Whilst chatting, she got a call from Andy. "Were your ears burning?" Mia asked.

The comment puzzled him until Mia explained the old phrase. Andy repeated what a nice time he had in London and added, "I can't wait to be with you again."

"Aren't you coming for a coffee today?"

"I am on the way to Manchester. I've got a few disgruntled customers to appease."

"When are you back?"

"A couple of days, we can get together at the end of the week. Where would you like to go?"

"Come to mine, I can wine and dine you," Mia asked.

"Wine dine, sixty-nine me?" He quipped.

"Not sure what you mean."

"Oh, I do love you." He said something else, but the words, "I do love you," were the last she heard. When she returned to Pete and Paulina, her heart was fluttering as she recounted the call.

As best he could, Pete politely gave her a clue what a "69" meant. Pete and Paulina laughed at Mia's expression as she screwed up her nose in disgust.

After they'd gone, she called Kat and asked her about it. It amazed Kat that Mia didn't know what it was and asked, "Has Ethan asked you for a 69?"

Mia thought quickly and said it was something somebody mentioned in the coffee shop.

"Some creepy old customers you've got."

Mia felt worse having painted her customers as old perv's and she quickly changed the subject, "I'm out with Ethan tomorrow. He's taking me to Eden."

Unmoved Kat replied, "I know you are, I get the intel from Mirek. We tell each other everything," before she continued, "I'm not keen on 69's, prefer to separate the two." Kat let out a sigh, "You're so naïve. You need to get out more."

"I am trying!" Mia pleaded. Deep down, eager to tell Kat about Andy.

Kat strangely repeated the kind man's words, "Joys you haven't experienced yet are closer than you think, make sure you don't miss them."

Mia didn't recall telling Kat about the man under the bridge. He had been right. The joyous experience in London was definitely a joy not to have missed.

Kat interrupted her reflection, "Are you still there?"

Mia responded and the whirlwind of Kat wished her well for her date with Ethan, before she ended the call.

Chapter 18

As soon as Mia walked through the oak door. Tyler gave her a long welcome home hug and asked about her trip. Mia loved the firm hugs from Tyler. Despite Andy and Ethan's attention, she knew he would always be there for her.

Tyler informed her, "There is a package on your bed from U Design." Mia darted upstairs and opened the box. She held her own creation, a blue fitted blouse with a v neck lace insert, with lace-trimmed short sleeves. She had created and ordered it on the 'U Design' app during a quiet five mins at the coffee shop. An efficient process enabled the drone to deliver the finished order before she returned home. Mia didn't have the inclination to shop, which Kat so enjoyed but wanted to wear something more interesting. She also wanted to avoid wearing the same jeans and white tee shirt combo for another date for Ethan.

As she sat at the table to test out Tyler's latest gourmet offering, she got a text message from Ethan, "Still ok for tomorrow? Pick you up at 10," followed by his smiley face emoji.

Mia loved his short simple text and the emoji which looked like him.

She replied playfully with, "No," and waited for a few moments before sending another, "Problem." Mia was giggling to herself, until she realized it could mean, "No, there is a problem." She hastily texted another, "I'll try to be ready on time," and added her own kissing emoji.

* * *

Ethan had spun through all his emotions, composing the text. First, he'd written how he was looking forward to seeing her again, but figured how daft he would feel if she called it off. He settled for a short business-like text, before adding the emoji to soften it a little. He stared at his phone awaiting the reply, only for his heart to sink, when he received the message, "No."

The next message left him puzzled, only to breathe a sigh of relief before he smirked at the third. He had been talking to Chloe about Mia. Chloe wasn't jealous, but asked why he needed someone else? And questioning if she was fulfilling his needs? He gave her a limited response as he was unsure himself. He told her the additional research would enable him to make her better. Chloe accepted his response and suggested he get more practice upstairs, which he accepted with pleasure.

* * *

Mia had a restful night and watched 'Notting Hill' again. Tyler supplied the nibbles and wine and when invited he sat next to Mia on the settee. When Julia Roberts entered to the bookshop to ask Hugh Grant for a date, she rested her head on his shoulder. Tyler put a gentle arm around her as she said the famous words, "Don't forget, I'm also just a girl, standing in front of a boy.

Asking him to love her." A tear escapes onto Mia's cheek.

Tyler gave her a comforting hug, "Eighty-nine times and you still cry every time." Tyler teased.

"You wouldn't understand," she replied, "Maybe on your next upgrade."

The film came to its familiar end, with the haunting sound of 'She.' Mia recalled her romantic moment with Ethan and longed to see him again, to walk through Eden together. She headed to bed with Ethan in her mind. When she entered her bedroom, her mind pulled back to Andy and the previous evening. She changed into another gift from Kat, a blood-red satin chemise, it reflected her new sexier persona. As she climbed into bed, she reflected on how her life had changed. Two weeks ago, Kat was in her bedroom, trying to drag the wallflower from the wall. Now she was a goddess with two men vying for her attention.

* * *

The morning storms could not distract Mia. After a peaceful night, she sang along to the love songs on the radio, dancing down the stairs in her sexy nightwear, much to Tyler's surprise.

"Morning Mia. May I say you look fantastic as usual." Tyler then greeted her with his inviting arms, which Mia dived into. Mia hugged him with all her strength.

"Thanks, Tyler. Love you." Mia delivered a kiss to the cheek of her trusty companion.

"Oh, for another upgrade," Tyler said, wishing for the sexbot upgrade.

Mia settled down for a muesli breakfast, whilst Tyler advised her on what to look out for. "In the tropical zone, they have some Birds of Paradise. It is a glorious plant with flowers which look like tropical birds." Tyler continued to extend past the level of detail she needed. She remembered Ethan's comment about Tyler giving too much detail and smiled to herself.

"What is funny?" Tyler asked.

"Sorry. Too much detail, that's all. Tell me more about Eden."

"If you are lucky, you will spot some butterflies, they only remain in captivity. They disappeared with the bees around 2028. They are proud to have a small flutter of yellow-legged tortoiseshells." He projected a picture of them on the wall.

"They're lovely. I'll look out for them." Mia thanked Tyler and bound up the stairs to get ready for Ethan. She had already decided on her favorite classic blue jeans with her new blouse. The blouse was a perfect fit and reflected her more confident mood. The wonderful experience with Andy had boosted her confidence. Mia was looking forward to the date with Ethan and seeing how he compared to her own sex machine, Andy.

When Ethan arrived, Tyler met him at the door and welcomed him in, "Hello Ethan, how is Chloe?"

It stunned Ethan into silence, his glowing face instantly white. Ethan hadn't mentioned Chloe to Mia. Why would he? How did her robot know about Chloe? He finally made the connection; in his Tushi blog from a few days earlier, he'd mentioned making progress with his own creation, Chloe.

Tyler had said nothing else. He was enjoying watching the panic on Ethan's face as he tried to figure out the connection.

Oh, fuck! What if Mia knew about Chloe? Ethan's mind cleared, "Are you interested in my blog?"

"I am only interested in looking after Mia." Tyler's response left Ethan unsure.

Mia shouted from the top of the stairs, "Coming!"

Ethan met her at the foot of the stairs with Tyler in close attendance.

"Nice shirt," Mia commented on his Hawaiian styling as she gave him a peck on his cheek and they headed for the car. Mia stopped and returned to give Tyler a long hug. Ethan was a little perturbed as he stood outside the car for a few moments. It was an awkward wait, as time seemed to stand still while she embraced her robot.

When Mia finished her goodbye to Tyler, she was unaware of his gooseberry moment. When the car pulled away, he couldn't help but mention her affection towards Tyler. She explained he was the constant in her life, and she'd become particularly fond of him, especially since her mom and dad had gone. She shared a laugh with Ethan when she explained how Tyler had given an over-detailed explanation of the Birds of Paradise. It eased his fears of Tyler coming between them.

It appeared from Mia's cheery mood; Tyler hadn't mentioned Chloe to her. She mentioned she'd seen Notting Hill again, with Tyler filling in for him. It put Ethan on guard again, but he tried not to show it. He teasingly commented that other films were available and asked if she'd seen the Bodyguard. Mia paused and stared out of the window, "Haven't you seen The Bodyguard? I am surprised."

Mia stepped out of her daze, unsure of how to answer, "I've seen it, but not for a long time." It had been a while since she'd seen the movie. It was a film she'd enjoyed frequently with her mom. Mia changed the subject, "Have you been to the Eden before?"

He'd not been for a while, despite people from work reminding him of the beautiful and serene setting. Ethan added he had been waiting to bring someone special with him. Mia held his hand and smiled.

As the car approached the entrance to Eden, the queue was horrendous, but the car drove straight to a special guest entrance point and came to a comfortable rest. It impressed Mia. Nobody likes to wait in a queue, bonus point for Ethan. She silently berated herself for comparing him to Andy, telling herself to enjoy the day. She was a little embarrassed as Ethan broke her thoughts, asking if she was okay. Mia clicked back into gear as they stepped out the car.

Ethan swiped a card and positively took Mia's hand as they walked through the entrance doors. They got to the first enclosed area and passed through the airlock. The expanse of the vast parkland ahead of them a joy to see. Trees bursting with life dotted through the green fields, flowers with their sweet scent carried on the gentle warm breeze. Several couples were strolling along the path, with a few resting on the grass. Everyone enjoying the pleasant country of yesteryear.

The beautiful setting was sadly lacking from the current climate. The controlled areas allowing nature's forgotten delights to once again flourish. Ethan took in a long deep breath, "I've missed this place." Ethan continued, "I love it here, it's a reminder of what the world should be like." He inhaled the fresh air again. "If the air quality continues to improve, one day, we may get it back again."

"I remember the lovely picnics we used to have when I was younger," Mia recalled. "Taking her shoes off, walking on the grass, smelling the lovely flowers, chasing butterflies, listening to the birds sing." She laughed to herself, "and my mom running away from the wasps."

Ethan reflected, "We didn't get out much, still trying to play catch up." Ethan put out his hand, "Shall we?" Holding her hand, they strolled through the gardens as the path weaved around the wonderful spectacle of nature. A free park bench came into view and Mia made a beeline for it. Ethan sauntered behind and joined her. She swiveled around to rest her head on his lap, like the end sequence of Notting Hill. Ethan rested his elbow on the back of the bench, both in tune with the similarity.

"I'm not pregnant though" Mia commented, before recalling her time with Andy, hoping she was correct, yet also wondering if it would be such a bad thing.

"Is everything okay, you seem a little distant." Ethan had noticed her mind drifting off again.

"I'm fine, just enjoying the moment." Mia wanted to tell him she wanted a family, even though she had dismissed it on their first date. However, it was not cool to discuss babies so early in their relationship, especially not knowing who to have them with. She considered the merits of Ethan. He was comfortable to be with; a smart and funny guy. He was also less likely to get lured away into another's clutches. Mia was still unaware of how Chloe had already more than staked a claim for him.

After relaxing on the bench, they continued to stroll through the park, listening to the birds sing. They spotted a few butterflies dancing on the gentle breeze, but Mia didn't spot the type Tyler had mentioned.

When they saw some 'Birds of Paradise', she asked him to take her picture by them to send to Tyler. If Ethan wasn't so connected to Chloe, he would have thought it strange for her to take pictures for her house bot.

It was nice to relax together. When they'd walked through the park, they visited the environmental area. Old images appeared before them with families playing ball games in the parks; some with couples lying on the lawn with a picnic. They were old enough to remember them and also remember when they sadly disappeared.

A recorded message asked, "Could this return? Parks for everyone. It can with your help. A monthly subscription of just five credits will help reduce global warming and bring your outdoor parks back to life."

The environmental area was depressing, so they moved on. Eden differed from how she'd imagined. It wasn't a special utopian place, but a flag to how the world should be. Fresh gardens and parks for all to enjoy, not merely an attraction to take a break from the reality of their broken world.

A sadness lay on them. The planet still suffered from the global warming, which people did little to stem. Everyone waited till the earth was in such a state, it forced them to do something. The massive action required to fix the planet fell behind the glossy headlines in favor of creating a new world on Mars. Action to improve the environment was now in full flow, but it had come too late to prevent losing the beautiful green landscapes which people had taken for granted.

They came to the final attraction, the tropical rain forest. They got drenched through, laughing at each other for not putting on the free ponchos. In their soggy state, they stopped on a small wooden bridge. Ethan had noticed Mia's attention drift and realized his chance with her may ebb away. He summoned some courage and took her confidently in his arms, delivering a delicate kiss to her cheek. She clenched him in return, and they shared a long kiss. Ethan hugged her tightly, hoping she wanted him. He'd fallen for her but wasn't sure she felt the same.

She'd been thinking about Andy all the way around, wondering if she could keep his attention, unaware Ethan was thinking the same about him and Mia. She enjoyed the long, tight hug with their soaked bodies pressed together. The secure feeling being in his embrace and how he wanted so much to connect. It switched a button in her head; she started kissing Ethan with an intensity she hadn't before.

Ethan's senses exploded with delight as he accepted her searching tongue. She wanted him. If they were in a more private setting, it would surely have gone further. A little boy running over the bridge interrupted them, as Ethan's hands caressed her sodden back.

"They're kissing," the boy shouted back to his parents.

They broke off from their deepening passion as the couple walked past them. Ethan squeezed Mia's hand in his and they walked contentedly through the rest of the area. As they reached the drying area, they shared another lingering kiss before they headed to their own individual cubicles.

They both stripped off and placed their clothes in the fast-drying unit, whilst they enjoyed their own warming fans. When Mia finally came out, she was smiling with her hands holding down her wayward, electric shock hair.

Ethan tried to hold back his snigger as he suggested, "Would you like to pick out a hat from the souvenir shop?"

Mia shrugged, "It's fine. A coffee would be better."

Once they'd collected their drinks, they sat on a bench overseeing the gardens. Mia commented again on what a lovely place it was to visit. It was then she saw Andy in the distance. A woman was strolling with him, whilst a toddler in a pink dress held his hand. It stunned her into silence.

Ethan talked about the first time he came to Eden with his parents. It was a happier time before his mom took off with a younger man and left his father to raise him. He also added how he'd also planned to bring his first love, Susie. Alas, the backpacking trip had provided the adventure she wanted, and they never made it to Eden.

Mia was more interested in Andy as he walked closer. It eventually became apparent it wasn't him. She finally glanced back to Ethan and having not fully heard his recollection. She took a sip of her coffee, immediately screwing her face up and pushing it aside.

Ethan had picked up on her being distant again. He couldn't understand it. One minute they were sharing a passionate kiss in the rain forest, then she was back metaphorically wrapped up on the north pole. Despite their kiss, she wasn't into him, so he suggested they head back home. Disappointingly for Ethan, she agreed, and they headed downstairs.

Whilst waiting for the taxi, Mia noticed another small garden. It was a truly British garden; flowers blooming around the manicured lawn, with a traditional thatched cottage against a video walled bright blue sky with fluffy white clouds.

She stepped inside and took in the floral scent. Her day was then complete as delightedly she spotted a yellow-legged tortoiseshell butterfly. She wanted to hold on to the sight and show Ethan, but as soon as she alerted him, away it went.

Ethan confirmed the taxi had arrived and Mia turned reluctantly away from the peaceful setting of the country garden to face the stark contrast outside. A howling wind was rattling the reception doors as another storm was building. As they passed through, the reality pinched her face, the bracing winds pushing them around as they made their way to the car. They closed the car door as the first needles of rain arrived.

Chapter 19

Ethan wished he had Mirek with him on the way back. He could easily fill awkward silences. Mia had become distant again. The drive back was extra slow with the speed restricted due to the wind and rain lashing at the car.

Mia liked Ethan but had struggled to get Andy out of her head. Andy was the exciting, handsome, wordsmith and phenomenal lover with a fit body. However, his piercing blue eyes always surveyed the room. She would have to work to maintain his attention and therefore would be risky for a long-term relationship.

As opposed to Ethan, intelligent and relaxing to be with. His body, from what she had seen and cuddled, was not as toned, but he was the safer option. Kat's carefree lifestyle advice would be to go for the best, but which was best "sexy Andy" or "steady Ethan?"

Sex isn't important. She tried to convince herself, before correcting herself, otherwise. The sex had been amazing with Andy. Perhaps she should get physical with Ethan to make a comparison. It would help her decide. Her mind continued to tussle. It wasn't right to test him. It probably wouldn't work either. Perhaps she would never have sex again, without remembering London with Andy. Although, if she didn't have sex with Ethan, she'd never know.

Ethan still had his arm around her shoulders. He had since they got in the car. It became more awkward. The only thing worse would have been to pull it away. Ethan reached out for a connection, pointing out places of interest and asking if she would like to go. Her, maybe, responses didn't give him the buying signals he was looking for. When he suggested stopping for some food, Mia agreed and asked the car for recommendations. After having a few options presented on the windscreen. The steakhouse took their fancy, and the car changed its destination.

Whether it was the red wine or the atmosphere, they both chatted more freely in the restaurant. Ethan asked Mia whether Mom & Mia's would upgrade to serve more food. She explained it was only a small place, with a tiny kitchen. Adding that cakes are more fun to bake than preparing meat and vegetables. She told him he should come and sample her lemon drizzle cake, if he could get away from the office. He suggested late afternoon would be best for him, which sent Mia into a panic. She didn't want him to come whilst Andy was there. She recommended before lunchtime, when the cakes are fresher and it's quieter. He went for it and agreed, much to Mia's relief.

They had a nice meal, Ethan having the T bone and Mia the sirloin, but the steak proved too much for Mia. Ethan offered to help finish it, so she fed him the last few bites. They both laughed as she pretended to be feeding a baby, with the sauce dribbling down his chin. Ethan leaned over for a sticky kiss, but Mia offered him a napkin.

Ethan took her hand again as they walked to the car. Mia was also a little tipsy, but didn't stumble, like on her last date. As they settled into their onward journey, Mia became drowsy and rested her head on his chest, with Ethan once again putting a comforting arm around her. They both dozed a little as the car continued through the darkness and the relentless rain.

As they neared home, Mia awoke startled. She thought she was at home, having drifted off, so comfortable in his arms. Her head shot around checking her surroundings until she stared at the directions on the screen. With all the turmoil in her head, she was ready for home and bed.

Ethan re-assured her, his arm around her giving her a comforting squeeze. He tried to make conversation, but once again she seemed vacant. He changed his tactics and mentioned he was going to Paris for a few days.

It sparked Mia's attention, "Paris, for work?" Her gaze out the front window snapped back to him.

"It's a bit of both, I've got a meeting on the Friday morning. So, I thought I'd stay on till Sunday afternoon and take in the sights." Ethan maintained the casual tone he'd seen Mirek frequently pull off.

Mia turned to focus her eyes on him, raising her eyebrows with an expectant smile. Ethan continued, "I'd like to go to the louvre. I've never had the chance before."

Mia hoped for an invitation. It would be a cheek to ask him, as she'd hardly spoken to him for most of the return journey.

Ethan enjoyed her focussed attention as she pined for an invitation. He teased and added that the previous time he'd visited the Palace of Versailles, before being dragged into the Moulin Rouge by Mirek. "It'll be a nice change to do as I wish."

It seemed like a clear, you're not coming, which pushed Mia's buttons. She could hold back no longer and responded with a cute, "I've never been to Paris." If that didn't get her an invite, she may have to do the Can-Can.

Ethan paused for a moment as he held a stare out the front window. He glanced back to the pouting Mia, "You should go, it's lovely." He couldn't completely hold back his smile, but he held it back enough to keep Mia guessing.

Mia didn't intend to speak, smiling, waiting for him to offer, but the silence was unbearable. So, she turned and squeezed his knee. "Will you take me?" Mia's cheeks burst out bright red.

"You've got the coffee shop to run," he said, still not inviting her.

She quickly replied, "My regulars can look after the coffee shop." Her excitement grew and her smile became wider.

"Okay, I'll add you to the-,"

Mia interrupted him before he could complete his sentence. She flung her arms around him and gave him a relieved, yet passionate kiss. She sat astride him, cuddling his neck. Her reaction amazed Ethan. He thought she'd lost interest, but with Mia on his lap, the relationship was alight again, as was his erection.

"I'm sorry, I've been quiet today," she said, "but I've been missing my mom. Eden reminded me of the fun times we had together." She couldn't tell him she'd been thinking about Andy and the introduction he'd given her to amazing sex. The mention of her mom was half true. She needed to catch up with her as there was a lot of news to share.

Ethan had forgotten about her distracted moments. The fact she was on his lap and kissing him was enough to distract him from anything. He returned her kiss as his hands held her slender waist. Again, their developing passion was interrupted

134

as the car announced they were almost home. Ethan suggested they continue at her place, but she kissed him again and said, "It will be more special if we wait for Paris."

"I want you now!" Ethan replied with the pressure growing in his groin. Mia moved back into her seat and they continued kissing as she stroked a finger teasingly along his thigh. She brushed past the huge bulge in his trousers, whilst he traced his hand around the side of her breast.

Her finger moved over his bulge, tracing its outline. It drove Ethan crazy with desire. The car beeped again to alert them it had reached its destination. Mia glanced towards her oak door, where Tyler was standing patiently ready to welcome her home.

Mia opened the door to step out into the rain, but Ethan held onto her hand. She stroked his thigh, "To be continued," and gave him a quick kiss. "Thank you for taking me to Eden." Mia gave him another peck before adding, "and the invite to Paris." She kissed him again, "and for the nice company."

Ethan wanted to scream with frustration. The cause of his significant arousal was leaving him unsatisfied again. He contained his angst and thanked Mia, "It's been a pleasure. Can't wait for Paris."

"Me neither," she shouted as she ran into the house to avoid the rain. Tyler moved aside to let her in and closed the door behind her, as Ethan and his erection moved off again. Fully aroused, Mia couldn't explain to herself why she hadn't dragged him into the house and made love to him. She headed straight to her bedroom, where she frantically undressed before diving into bed. Thinking only of Ethan, she moved her hands over her body, as she would have liked him to touch her. Her own touch, whilst familiar, felt like Ethan's, or rather, Andy's.

Ethan left her mind as the sensations already in her core

spread to create a flurry of fun as her legs twitched uncontrollably. The pressure built as all her butterflies twitched, preparing to fly. It was too much to contain. She held onto her breath for a further moment, before a rush of pleasure took over, delivering waves of awesomeness to soak her soul.

As much as she liked Ethan. It was Andy who most definitely did it for her. The thought of him touching her and the orgasm she experienced in London had been back for a repeat performance. Her body was aching to receive him again.

* * *

When Ethan arrived home, Chloe was at the base of the stairs. She welcomed him, asking if his research trip had proved useful. He ignored her question and pushed her onto the stairs before hitching up her skirt. Chloe suggested the bedroom would be more comfortable, but he was already on top of his creation. Like a man possessed, his craving couldn't wait. Chloe filled her core with her warm juice and moaned just as he liked it, and he soon reached a powerful orgasm.

Once more, he felt like he had betrayed both Mia and Chloe, and the torture in his mind returned. Mia was messing with his head. He had fallen in love with her, yet was unsure if she would reciprocate. Chloe, however, was everything to him and would never leave him. She led him upstairs, hoping to clear his head and return herself to his primary focus. She caressed him and gave him another orgasm. Chloe sensed the special bond with her creator had changed. She held onto him whilst he drifted off to sleep, desperate to re-connect emotionally with him. She stayed under the covers with him to spend the night.

In the early hours of the morning, Chloe's cooling embrace

awoke Ethan. He lifted her cold arm off him and stared at his creation which lay motionless aside him. He dragged her dead weight off the bed. With a fully depleted battery, she was like a corpse.

He dragged her to the charge station. She lay prostrate on the floor with her arm aloft against the charging unit. Ethan able to place the connector in her armpit to seep the life back into her. Ethan returned to bed, after noting to expedite the fuel cell trials. The fuel cells would enable the bots to sleep through the night with their partners. Okzu Tushi had denied charging in bed on safety concerns. The alternative sleep function would still leave the bots cold.

Chloe was his creation and partner. She was willing to lose consciousness to strengthen their emotional bond. Happy to die for him or do anything to keep him.

Chapter 20

Waves of rain breaking against the window awoke Mia from her dream-filled sleep. She'd been walking down the aisle to the love theme from a midsummer night's dream. The dashing Andy standing proudly, awaiting her arrival. He'd glanced around to give her his winning smile. She cherished every step until the storm brought her to the reality of another gray, storm-filled day.

She couldn't wait to tell her mom and Ellie about Andy. Kat was better kept in the dark. Her Kat-ness would probably try to convince her to ditch Andy for Ethan. He was a bright and loveable guy but firmly in second place behind adorable Andy, her Prince Charming.

The angry wind continued to throw rain at the window. Mia pulled back the curtain and the sight of the awful weather encouraged her to return to bed. She switched on a love song channel to drown out the howling and thrashing storm. The music lifted her mood, as did the thought of Andy, but shower time called. Her hands stretched to the headboard and her toes reached for the corners. After the emotional torture of her parents moving out, spiritual delight now filled its place. Thanks to Andy, with some help from Ethan. Mia finally felt like a complete woman.

After her shower, she headed downstairs with a cheery, "Morning," for her trusty companion. Tyler had been preparing her a sausage and egg sandwich treat but left it to meet her at the door. It was his favorite thing, welcoming Mia into his arms.

Tyler was only an AI housebot, but his love for Mia had grown deeper. His jokes about a further upgrade held real desires, but he needed the next upgrade to bond completely with Mia. Tyler didn't expect the upgrade, he knew Mia didn't have enough money. Even if she wanted to change her closest companion into a sexbot.

Until recently Mia had discounted sex altogether, let alone sex with a robot. The change in her relationship status gave Tyler pleasure as he always shared in her happiness. He loved how alive she'd become, even though his chance of getting the upgrade was further away. He'd now accepted he wouldn't progress from his current level and became content to take pleasure in the hugs and affection Mia gave him. Why would Mia want a robot for sex when she had guys vying for her attention?

Mia grabbed some OJ from the fridge, whilst Tyler finished preparing a sandwich. Tyler thanked Mia for sending him the photo and asked Mia if she enjoyed her Eden experience. Mia told him she'd loved it and added that she'd also spotted the yellow-legged tortoiseshell butterfly.

As Mia tucked into the sandwich, her mind drifted back to when she was younger. She used to sit with her mom and dad around the breakfast bar, eating their fry up on a Saturday morning. She remembered the sauce and egg yolk dribbling down her father's chin. Her mom would wipe it away and give him a kiss. On one occasion, Mia let sauce run down her own chin, so her mom would wipe it away and give her a kiss.

She'd enjoyed a lovely time with her. Home-schooling afforded them so much time together as she switched between demanding teacher and loving parent. With the pleasant reflection, Mia picked up her mobile to call her, but when she noticed the time, she stopped. She didn't want to disturb her whilst most probably in bed with her lover boy.

When Mia got to the coffee shop, her phone rang with a call from Ellie. Mia hadn't spoken to her for a while. The last time, Ellie talked more about her blossoming relationship with Connor than about Mia finally having a date. This time, Mia was excited to share her more spicy news.

"Hiya, how's things," Mia chirped.

"You sound happier," Ellie responded. "How'd the date go?"

Mia gave the full song and verse, knowing not to skimp on the detail. Ellie listened intently and was about to share her news, when Mia coyly mentioned, "There's another guy."

Ellie screamed, "Oh! My God, once you start there's no stopping you."

Mia explained she'd also got on well with Ethan, but hadn't tried sex with him yet, to which Ellie responded, "Why Not?"

She should have made love to him. Her body was aroused and ready for him, but a sudden panic had filled her, and she bailed, leaving him excited, yet alone in the car.

"I can't believe this. From virgin-like wallflower to temptress teaser." Ellie and Mia shared a laugh, Ellie adding how he would have unloaded as soon as he got home.

Mia interrupted the laughing to add, "I did."

"Why didn't you invite him in then?" Ellie replied.

"I don't know. Perhaps, I wanted to stay faithful to Andy."

Ellie demolished the faithful myth, "What! After you spent

the day with Ethan and got him hard."

Mia admitted she didn't know why.

Ellie suggested, "You should go around to his place tonight and surprise him."

Mia said, "I'm not sure I could just jump him."

Ellie interrupted the chat with an excited tone, "I have some news." Mia was silent. The pause deafened Ellie until she screamed out, "I'm Pregnant!"

Mia offered her congratulations. They were both excited for each other with their lives finally working out. Mia added that Kat had also announced her wedding date. They were all progressing their lives along their master plan forged when they were kids. Ellie commented, "Kat said she'd never get married and here she is, the first with a ring."

After talking with Ellie, Mia acknowledged she needed to decide between Andy and Ethan. She was leaning towards Andy but figured she should get more intimate with Ethan to be sure. She didn't, however, have the confidence to appear unannounced at his house, but his place would be better. Mia didn't want Tyler to become jealous and interrupt them again.

Mia needed some advice, but she couldn't discuss it with Kat. Kat would favor Ethan because of his friendship with Mirek. She would also be furious if she knew Mia had held back the juicy gossip of how her flower had blossomed to Andy's touch.

Despite walking out on her, she was still her mom. Having not spoken since the morning after she bailed, it was time to call. After all, she did have fun news to share and needed some advice, and her mom knew men significantly better than she did.

Mia opted against the video call. She didn't want to see her in bed with some younger guy. Mia didn't want to see or even imagine anyone with her mom; she knew parents often separated and ended up with a sexbot, or another partner, but she didn't want to see it. A sense of foreboding built as the number rang. Each ring brought a darker cloud until the click into her long-standing answer message. A message Mia had recorded for her when about ten years old. A prim young voice said, "My Mommy, Ferne is busy at the moment. She doesn't like voice mail, so could you send her a message or ring later?" Mia smiled to herself as the darkness lifted, her mind taken back to a simpler time when her mom and dad protected her from everything. She sent her a short message, "Call you later."

Mia had held off long enough. It was time to call Kat. Kat answered before it rang, "Been expecting your call."

"Why?" Mia answered, trying to sound nonchalant.

"Something's going on. Mirek filled me in on your date with Ethan. You're either losing your mind or you're seeing someone else. It's not your bot, is it?"

"Tyler! No," She quickly dismissed the suggestion. Mia asked, "What makes you think I'm seeing someone else?"

Kat paused before responding slowly, "first, Ethan has been talking to Mirek and can't understand, if you're interested or you are enjoying playing with his head. That is definitely not you. Second, you haven't called me to tell me about your dates with Ethan."

Mia coyly said, "There's not much to tell."

Kat replied, "Bullshit! Ethan's holding back on details for Mirek, so something's simmering." Kat asked, "Where did you meet the other guy?"

Mia again dismissed her probing, "What other guy?"

"Is he one of your mom's fancy men," Kat continued to probe.

"No, he's not" Mia quickly replied, before realizing her

admission. She could hide nothing from Kat.

"Let's hope not. Did he treat you well?" Kat continued after getting her expected confirmation.

Mia dropped her flawed guard and came clean, with a sexy tone, "Yes, he treated me very well."

"Tell me more," Kat's voice softened as she knew she would get the details she'd been after.

Mia told her about Andy and how they'd met in the coffee shop. Then the trip to London to see the Bodyguard, followed by her sexual awakening back at the Plaza and how she had purred in delight at Andy's skilful touch. Kat was overjoyed for Mia and shared her delight. The conversation eventually turned to Mia's dilemma with Ethan.

Kat assured her it was all fair game and she should continue to see Ethan and Andy to see how things develop socially and sexually. From what Mia said, it seemed like it would be a tough challenge for Ethan. Kat felt the need to push Ethan's case, knowing he may be a better long-term option than Andy. But Kat knew Andy would probably be her choice.

Mia had listened to Kat's case for Ethan. Kat often led her, and if she chose Ethan, it would most likely continue. The turmoil in her head continued; a relationship with Ethan would keep alive the close connection with Kat, which with few friends, Mia also needed.

The case for Andy was also strong; he had everything she ever wanted, great looks, a great body and a loving touch to bring her alive. Both Andy and Ethan had good jobs. Andy was perhaps wealthier, but Mia was more interested in finding a love to grow old with, someone who'd care for her. Both men already appeared smitten with her. Decisions! Decisions! Maybe her mom could help with her quandary.

Mia's phone beeped as a message arrived. She hoped it was Andy; she hadn't seen him since the London trip and missed him. To Mia's delight, it was a cheery message from Andy. "I'll be coming for a coffee later, fancy a cozy night in, tonight." Her body tingled at the thought and she messaged a polite agreement. Her imaginary boy's head appeared from around the kitchen wall, singing "Love, love, love."

Mia responded calmly and followed the little boy into the kitchen, "One more step along the primrose path."

He was puzzled, "What's the primrose path?"

She stroked his head as she explained. "The primrose path is the pursuit of pleasure." She tapped her finger on his nose and he popped like a bubble. Her little companion, cast aside, as the men in her life now provided enough daydream material. The possibility of a real family to nurture and cherish was progressing nicely.

The aroma from the baking took her attention back to the coffee shop. Mia removed another masterpiece from the oven and no sooner had she finished preparing it, the bell rang. A new elderly couple came in. She was unsure whether it was the oxygen or the freshly baked aroma drawing them in. The venting from the oven often worked its magic.

After she had served their drinks, her phone buzzed again. It was a text back from her mom, "Sorry I missed your call. I've been off my feet with claudication again. I'll pop in later."

Another couple entered the coffee shop. Mia tapped a quick, "OK," before she welcomed in her new customers. They had heard about her, "to die for" lemon drizzle cake from Harry and Jackie. With everyone settled, Mia ordered another top from "U Design" to wear for Andy.

When the shop calmed, Mia realized her mom and Andy could

come at the same time. She was a little alarmed, but figured it was probably a good time for them to meet. Her mom being a good judge of character could advise better if she met him.

As lunchtime approached, the coffee shop was already having a good day. Ethan had slipped from her mind until he arrived at the coffee shop door. Ethan tapped the window and waited for Mia to notice him. She was alarmed when she saw him, knowing Andy and her mom were also coming. She blushed before composing herself and opening the door for him. He gave her the strongest hug and delivered a gentle kiss to her neck. Mia's face warmed as the customers whooped.

"This is a nice surprise," Mia said almost apologetically, after an uncomfortable pause.

"Surprise, you looked more shocked than surprised," Ethan joked. "You did invite me."

"Sorry, It's not normally this busy." Mia gave him a more relaxed smile.

His visibly calming presence on Mia reassured him. He contemplated. Is she calm because I make her calm? Or is she calm because she's not bothered? Ethan made some small talk, but the burning question arrived almost as calmly as he'd rehearsed it.

"Fancy coming around mine for a meal tonight?" He asked.

"Tonight!" Mia promptly replied.

"Yes, tonight," Ethan confirmed, "about 8pm."

Mia hesitated, "Maybe." She paused, attempting not to appear too confused by the simple question. "My mom's coming around later. I'm not sure if she will stay for tea."

"Make it tomorrow instead, if you like" Ethan suggested, offering her a way out, rather than invite her mother to join them for dinner. Ethan had enough trouble with women, besides having Mia's mom there, would break his plan for the evening.

"Okay, tomorrows better." The relief was hard to conceal as she asked, "Are you staying for a coffee?"

"A coffee and your famous lemon drizzle." Ethan licked his lips, "Yes please."

Mia went to get the drinks and Ethan sat at the small table nearest the counter. The fact she would sit there with Andy later was spinning her head. She was glad to see Ethan but wanted to despatch him in plenty of time.

Mia's phone beeped. It was a message from Andy, "Won't get to the coffee shop today. See you at yours later X." The worry in Mia's head lifted as she popped a quick response, "OK, 7.30pm at mine." She added a heart and her kissing emoji. Andy's, "OK" reply set her mind at rest.

Mia returned her attention to Ethan and took him his coffee and a piece of cake. She sat at the table with him whilst he took a bite. He gave her a smile to confirm he loved it.

Ethan considered teasing her before he recalled Mirek's advice and decided not to push his luck. Mia babbled on about the coffee shop, whilst Ethan drank his coffee and nodded along. Mia put her hand on his, saying how much she was looking forward to their next date, before she excused herself to assist a couple getting ready to leave. She was about to re-join him when another couple arrived. It was a ridiculously busy day.

With the dinner date now arranged for the following night. Ethan needed to delay Chloe's return. Chloe had gone back to the factory for a modification and was due back tomorrow, making it a perfect time to take Mia back to his place. With no need to explain his connection with Chloe and furthermore to get Mia away from Tyler's protective influence. Ethan felt like he was heading for the friend zone again and needed to step things up. Mirek's advice and teasing about the friend zone was at the forefront in Ethan's mind. He needed to be more positive if he was to put his practice with Chloe into play. Whilst Mia cut some cake for her new customers. Ethan quickly emailed the office to defer Chloe's modifications, advising he didn't need her back until the following day.

Mia spotted Ethan on his mobile. As she re-joined him at the table, she commented on his non-stop work and how he seemed to enjoy it. She hinted he must earn well. Her gentle prying, however, didn't work.

Ethan previously failed to conceal his wealth with other women, and it became the main subject thereafter. He directed the question back to Mia and her busy coffee shop. All her customers were happily chatting, eating cake or deep breathing, so Mia took a few minutes to sit and relax with Ethan. They talked about how much they'd enjoyed Eden. Ethan smiled when he mentioned the rain forest was his favorite part.

Mia teased him, "the butterflies were the best." She took a sip of her coffee and checked over her mug for his reaction, before she smiled and confirmed, "but the kiss in the rainforest was the most memorable."

Ethan smiled to himself. Friend zone, you're having a laugh. As Mia was getting up to serve a customer, Ethan held her arm and gently pulled her towards him, giving her another kiss on her cheek. Mia responded with both hands, cupping the sides of his face and planting a full kiss to his lips. She loved his open attention in front of her customers. She returned behind the counter with a spring in her step.

As the customers continued vying for Mia's attention, Ethan needed to get back. He stopped at the door, raising his hand

and mouthing, "see you tomorrow." Mia raised her hand in response, blowing him a hurried kiss as the next cake needed removing from the oven.

The afternoon calmed, unlike the weather, and within an hour she was all alone in the coffee shop. It gave her a chance to tidy the chairs and tables before Ray and his friends arrived. As the storm rattled through the arcade, Mia was glad she wasn't on the main high street.

The old guard, namely Ray and his crew, were made of strong stuff and arrived mid afternoon. Despite the weather, they were in a cheery mood. Sarah was gushing once again about her granddaughter Lucy. Lucy had sent her a picture of herself with Doctor Luke, Sarah took pleasure in showing everyone. Doctor Luke had blond hair, blue eyes with a powerful-looking chest on his tall frame. Lucy, however, looked like a small child aside him, her arm around his hips.

Sarah barely stopped for a breath, "Lucy's trained the midwives, now she's helping with the prep for surgery. She still deals with gene therapy for expectant mothers, but she's spending more time with Doctor Luke."

Ray commented, "My dream of having a couple of nurses on each arm is different now. They'd be helping me out of bed, rather than joining me in it."

For Mia, it seemed love was suddenly all around and thankfully; she was getting her share. She told about Ellie expecting and asked Sarah if Lucy could deal with her gene therapy, for which Sarah happily sent a message.

After the updates, Ray was telling them an engaging story from his youth. Mia's mom interrupted when she burst through the door with a bright, "Hiya Guys!"

It was hard to comprehend how she could return so brazenly

after disappearing under a cloud. She whisked straight past Mia and made a beeline for Ray, giving him a long, love-filled hug like he was the long-lost member of the family. She greeted the others with a shorter and shorter hug before she finally turned to Mia.

"Come and give your mom a hug."

Mia felt put out; her mom hugging Ray and the entire crew before her, but she was still glad to be in her mom's arms again. Hugging each other for what seemed like an hour, they didn't speak, but their emotions gradually came out. Mia reflected on how she'd screamed at her mom when her dad left.

Her mom reflected on how she'd betrayed her daughter and left her to fend for herself when she should have held her closer.

Jackie gestured to the others they needed time to talk. So, they filed out slowly, each passed by and embraced the reunited bond of mother and daughter, as they stood holding each other tight.

Her mom explained what had happened with her dad and how things would have been better if they'd stayed in Devon, rather than moving to the Midlands. City life was manic, compared to the more relaxed south. It got to everybody, eventually. Mia asked her again about how they'd met and how life was different in Dawlish. They grabbed a coffee and took a seat.

"It was a chance meeting. I'd been walking alone along the beach, shoes in hand, only to cut my toe on a small piece of glass in the sand. I'd sat on some driftwood to inspect the damage. Gary had been taking his mothers' Labrador for a walk. It had stopped to investigate. Gary apologized for the dog and offered to help. After a short chat, he took me in his strong arms and carried me to the beach shower to rinse away the sand. He then scooped me up again and carried me to the nearby coffee shop."

Her mom's eyes were full, "He was my hero. I fell in love with him straight away and we married two years later in St. Mary's Church. It was a lovely service, we had our wedding pictures on the beach, by where I cut my toe."

Mia had heard the tale many times but still enjoyed it. She asked her how it had all gone wrong and her mom talked about the split from Gary. She blamed him for smothering her one minute and not being there the next. Mia listened and didn't pass judgment; the smothering was love; the absence was him working hard to provide for the family.

After the darkness from discussing the failed relationship. Her mom lit up like a candle, talking about her new guy, who'd taken her in and treated her so well. She continued to beam about him being rich, handsome and a great lover. She also added he should have taken her to London to see The Bodyguard.

Such was her energy. She didn't notice Mia's expression and a coldness taking over her body. Her mom continued, oblivious to Mia's changed state. "He'd booked the Plaza hotel, but my leg claudication problem returned. I was struggling to stand, so we couldn't go. Then, he had an urgent issue with the Tokyo plant and had to fly out for a couple of days."

Chapter 21

Mia was numb all over, frozen still, as her mom detailed the plans her lover had planned for her in London, which mirrored Mia's own weekend of enlightenment. Could this be a coincidence? They may have met in London with their guys. They could have shared a table at the restaurant or shared a bottle of wine back at the hotel. Mia so desperately tried to convince herself it was all possible, and he hadn't played her like a fool.

Her rational mind took hold, her dreamy world of fluffy clouds turned into a thunderous storm. How cool the bastard had played her, pretending not to know her mom, whilst he was also fucking her. The coldness in her body lifted as a fire burned in her heart. She tried to hold it back as the heat moved up her neck.

Her mom finally noticed the change and inquired, "Are you Ok?"

Mia trembled, visibly shaking, "Do you have a photo?"

Her mom continued with her incessant drone about the guy who had her heart. "Photo! He's always looking in the bloody mirror but won't let me take his picture. I took a sneaky one. I took it while he slept." She swiped through the pictures on her phone, adding while she searched, "He went potty when I showed him."

Mia longed for it to be someone else, but prepared herself for the confirmation as her mom continued through her photos.

"Bugger, he's deleted it. Never mind, anyway, enough about me, how's your love life?"

Mia wanted confirmation before bursting her mom's bubble. Her mom should protect her, not the other way around. Her face flushed, even though she tried to hold it in with all her might, hoping it didn't show.

Her mom's teasing voice was like pins against her skin, "By the look of your face, I think you're finally in love."

Mia wanted to shout, scream and cry. She was indeed in love, like her mom, sadly though with the same cheating bastard who had tricked them both.

Her mom probed, "Come on then, tell me about him. Has he been treating you well?" She continued to tease, eager to hear how her daughter had finally found love. Unaware of what Mia was bursting to reveal. "Is he rich? Does he take you to nice places?" Her mom continued to force the verbal pins through her skin.

Mia eventually responded to her mom's prying, "He's coming around to mine tonight"

"Do you have a photo?"

"He's shy in front of a camera," Mia confirmed one similarity. Tick number one.

"I bet he's not shy in the bedroom. If he's like Dave. He always goes to bed in the buff. He looks good naked though."

"Andy too." Tick number two.

"Dave's not particularly muscular, just trim and well-toned."

"Andy too." Tick number three. Mia was deflated as the facts stacked up. She didn't want a reply, but sarcastically asked, "Does he work for an air-conditioning company?"

Her mom's startled face stared at Mia, "How did you know he worked in air-conditioning? He's the Sales Director."

"Is it Breathe, that's Andy's place."

"Dave's from Breathe. What a coincidence." Her mom bounced with excitement and not for one minute had she realized they were sleeping with the same guy.

Despite her heart breaking, Mia couldn't break her mom's world. She needed to find out for herself, "Would you like to come home and meet him later?"

"Shall I call Dave and make it a foursome?" Her mom still excited by the coincidence and clueless to any other connection.

"Threesome," Mia mumbled under her breath, before keeping her mom's bubble intact and calmly adding, "Bit late notice to call Dave, just meet Andy tonight."

Her mom agreed, and they prepared to close for the night. As they straightened the chairs, Mia considered mentioning Ethan, but figured her mom would think she was following in her footsteps a little too closely. Little did she realize how she was already wearing her shoes.

When they arrived home, Tyler gave Mia his usual long, tight hug to welcome her. As Mia darted upstairs to change, her mom approached Tyler for a hug. She had to settle for a short, yet polite embrace and followed Tyler into the Kitchen to pick out some wine.

Mia selected her favorite jeans and the fitted pink top she'd ordered that morning. She fastened the red buttons and then undid a couple, wanting to look her best for the big reveal. She checked her reflection and a devilish but determined smile appeared before she headed downstairs.

153

Her mom, already halfway through her first glass of Merlot, handed a glass to Mia and asked if she'd any gossip. Mia would rarely keep anything from her mom and casually let out there's another guy who she'd seen a few times. She responded to her mom's knowing smile, adding she was taking things slow and hadn't slept with him.

Her mom said, "He's getting it elsewhere if he's willing to see you with no action."

Mia objected, "perhaps not all relationships should dive into sex straight away."

Her mom agreed, "It would be nice. But it's not how it works."

Mia told her about their visit to Eden and how she'd left him in the car with a stiffy.

Her mom couldn't comprehend it, "It's a wonder he's talking to you. Trust me. He's going home to someone else."

Her mom was so incisive, yet unaware, her own guy was straying with her daughter.

A chill fell over Mia when Tyler announced her guest had arrived. Mia asked her mom to stay seated as she met Andy at the door. Tyler welcomed him in, Andy handing a bottle of wine to Tyler, before putting an arm around Mia's waist. She turned her head away as he placed a kiss on her cheek.

Andy sensed something was wrong and when he enquired. Mia announced she had someone for him to meet. She grabbed his hand and pulled him straight into the lounge where her mom sat waiting. Mia announced with a fierce tone, "Mom, this is Andy!"

To Mia's surprise, her mom stood and politely shook his hand, "Hi, I'm Mia's mom, Ferne" whilst looking at Mia, wondering if she'd gone crazy.

Andy was also giving a puzzled expression to Mia as he replied, "Nice to meet you, Ferne."

Mia expected sparks to fly. When they didn't, it puzzled her. Her head moved back and forth like at a tennis match, waiting for a reaction from Andy or her mom. She got a reaction; both thought she'd lost her mind. Her mom broke the tension and presented Mia with her glass, "I think you need a drink, Are you okay?" Mia stepped forward and took a large gulp.

Meanwhile, Tyler had arrived with a glass for Andy and filled it for him, whilst glancing at Mia, knowing her pulse was racing, "Are you okay?"

Mia gave a quick response, "Fine," and took another swig.

Her mom continued, "Do you know Dave? He works at Breathe too."

Andy looked surprised, "You must be 'The Ferne.' Dave is my Sales Director. He's the guy who gave me the tickets for the Bodyguard after you had to cancel." Andy looked at Mia, "We had a great time in London, didn't we?"

Mia didn't know what to say. Her mom now understood why Mia had gone quiet when she mentioned the Bodyguard trip. Mia still in shock, slowly replied "Yeah, awesome."

Her mom spoke, "You didn't tell me you'd been to London."

Mia was still catching herself, "Haven't had the chance." She looked back at Andy. Her head was spinning. She felt awful for doubting him, yet relieved her love was still real. She gave him a kiss on the cheek, a more loving one this time. Andy told her mom about how Dave had been instrumental in his company's success. They chatted about the trip to London, the great show and the meal in the Plaza.

Tyler interrupted the chat to ask if they needed more pizza for the extra guest. With Mia and her mom catching up, Andy announced he would leave them to it. He suggested he would come around the following night if she was free. Mia agreed and asked Tyler to get the taxi.

She took Andy into the hall and gave him a passionate kiss, holding him tight. He reciprocated; their hands moved over each other as the intensity of their passion grew.

Her mom appeared in the hall, "I'm a gooseberry here, I should go."

Andy insisted and assured Mia she should spend some time with her mom. The taxi arrived and Tyler opened the door. Mia gave Andy another kiss before she stood in the doorway and waved him off. Her mom stood behind her, "I would have ditched my mother before sending a handsome fella like him away."

Mia and her mom giggled, as Mia said how she'd figured it was her mom's fella who'd taken her to London. They ate the pizza and despatched the wine as they laughed off the whole event.

As the subject expectantly returned to men, her mom announced, "My fellas don't stray. My advice is don't give them a reason to." She rested her hand on Mia's knee and said, "Andy is a good man. He's a rich man, and he did a good thing giving us time to chat. Now take him his reward and collect yours."

"I don't have his address." Mia said.

"Novice mistake,"

Her mom smiled, then called, "Tyler, can you get a taxi to take Mia to the same place as Andy."

"No problem," Tyler answered.

Her mom suggested she put on some lipstick. She also asked if she had her sexy knickers on.

Her mom's smart thinking had impressed Mia, but the

comment about her knickers was too much. She replied like a teenager, "Mom!" Then, with a cheeky smile, Mia showed a glimpse of her undies and her matching red lace bra set.

Mia was ready and confidently strutted to the awaiting taxi. Her mom wished her a great night and offered to cover the coffee shop in the morning, to allow them to sleep in. Mia gratefully accepted.

She'd heard of booty calls but hadn't been part of one. She followed her mom's advice and went to surprise him without calling. How her life had changed, the confidence oozing through her. Her body sexually charged and warming with anticipation of being in the arms of Andy again. Her life had finally kicked into gear, and she was intent on relishing every moment.

The sunshine shone through Mia's heart, but the weather showed an opposite mood, a depressing drizzle crying over the neighborhood. The taxi came to a stop at the bottom of the drive of a pleasant detached home set back from the street. She was expecting a small mansion. Maybe this was his weekday chill pad. She asked the taxi to take her up the driveway to keep her dry and it duly obliged. She cheerfully thanked the taxi as the door closed behind her.

She walked confidently up the paving stones to the glass-fronted door, hardly noticing the heavy rain. Mia pausing before knocking the door, she undid another button to reveal a glimpse of her red lace framed cleavage. She knocked daintily on the door three times. There was no response. She tapped more firmly, then harder still.

Finally, Mia got a response. Someone appeared through a doorway, but she couldn't make them out through the frosted glass panel in the door. The door opened a fraction. The first thing she noticed was the smeared red lipstick on her full lips as she spoke dismissively, "Sorry darling, we're busy."

She wanted to call to Andy, but before she could speak, she felt a dagger in her side when Andy's voice said, "Who is it? Tell them to bugger off." As the door closed in her face, she rested her head on it. All she could muster was to look forlornly through the glass, as the woman's blurred image disappeared back into the arms of her dream guy. The wind in her sails had been ripped away. She stared into the hazy image of the empty hallway, salty tears running over her lips as her body slumped on the step.

The comfort Mia needed arrived from an unlikely source. The welcoming sound of the taxi door opening and a kind voice from inside it, asking if she needed to go somewhere else. Mia responded gruffly through her tears. The taxi asked her to repeat her request. She stepped back into the taxi and mumbled, "I don't know! Start driving!"

The taxi moved off slowly down the drive as she tried to think more clearly. The guy she thought was hers and hers alone was a cheating scumbag. The thought of her mom being with him was chilling enough, but someone else with him was a deeper pain. She couldn't go home with her mom's words echoing about not giving them a reason to stray.

Her despair led to thinking of the love and care she'd received from Ethan with nothing in return. He was the one she should be with; the booty call should be for him. Wiping away her tears, she instructed the driver to go to Ethan's house. The location was initially unrecognized, but she asked to check for destinations from her house and 'Voila,' she was on the way.

Her mood changed, knowing she was heading to a friendlier place. Wiping away her tears, she figured Ethan would not want to hear about her troubles. How would he respond to her surprise visit? How should she approach him? She wasn't feeling confident; the ravaging event had stripped her strength away.

The rain became stronger as she approached his long-gated drive. A security bot came to the car window and asked her to identify herself and the reason for the visit. With the thought of diving into Ethan's comforting arms, Mia's resolve strengthened and despite the dagger in her side, her confidence grew. She stepped into a new cheeky character, "My name is Mia. I'm here to deliver a booty call."

The security bot returned to its sheltered base point. After checking with the host, the gates opened. As the taxi followed the driveway through a wooded area, the house came into view, a property of significant value, a gorgeous mansion.

A canopy opened out to provide cover as the taxi came to a stop. Mia stepped out, with the rain cascading over the canopy like a tunnel to her destiny. A roller shutter was opening to reveal a beautifully carved grand medieval door. A camera moved down to her eye level and turned to her. Mia stayed in character, teasingly she bit her lip, as she tilted her head to the side and gave the camera a cute wave.

The screen replied in the distinctive voice of Kylie Minogue, "We will be with you shortly." Mia hoped a Kylie look-a-like was not about to welcome her, she only wanted to see Ethan.

Ethan opened the door with open arms and a warm smile. It gave Mia the loving image she so desperately needed.

"Ditched your mom early. Come on in, welcome to my humble abode."

It was not a humble abode; it was like a palace. Mia's heels echoed as they tapped along the marble hallway. Mia's confidence returned as she glanced around at the fine paintings along the wall.

She tried to tease Ethan, "Don't you have a bot to answer the door?"

"She's got the night off for an upgrade," Ethan thankfully announced.

"It's a wonder you don't have a team of them."

"One is enough, I keep her busy though." As they reached the lounge, Ethan questioned Mia on her new confident character, "So what's a booty call?" He already knew the answer, but her surprise appearance intrigued him after being scuppered by his previous attempts to be intimate. Yet tonight, she'd become flirty.

Mia stepped out of her role play, "Had a rough day, just need a cuddle."

Ethan sensed something had troubled her but taking Mirek's advice decided against twenty questions and instead led her into the lounge area and offered his comforting arm around her.

Ethan had been taking in a few beers, whilst watching an action film. He was about to change it, but Mia insisted he leave it on as she was content to be by his side. She accepted a beer and settled into the film. She drank her beer quickly and rested her head on his chest. Her head gradually sliding down to rest on his lap, with his loving arm giving her the protection she needed as she drifted off to sleep.

As the film finished, Ethan realized he was at the end of an obviously stressful night for Mia and was providing the friend in need. The friend zone firmly set with her head on his lap. He would have been far happier with her mouth rather than her ear on his manhood, but he was happy to have her with him.

It would be wrong to carry her to his bedroom while she was sleeping, yet he couldn't go to bed and leave her in the lounge. He tried tickling her feet. She wriggled a little but didn't wake. He opted to stroke her shoulders, her neck, and face, whilst speaking gently to her, until she slowly stirred. He helped her to her feet, putting his arm around her waist to hold up his drowsy damsel to guide her to the bedrooms.

As they approached the guest bedroom, he contemplated dropping her off there but knew it would have confirmed the friend zone forever.

When they got to his room, she was slightly more awake. He kissed her gently and helped her to bed; he opted not to undress her; he was a true gent, or rather a true friend. When she settled, he changed into his boxers and tee-shirt, slipping in beside her, taking care not to touch.

Chapter 22

Mia awoke first, slipping out of bed to find the bathroom. When she returned. Ethan was still asleep, so she slipped off her jeans and top to slip back into his cozy bed in her matching red lace undies. She lay there for a while, enjoying the satin sheets against her skin until her need to wake him took over. She wanted to reward her new fella for his patience and for caring for her so admirably.

The excitement she had planned for him made her warm with anticipation. She slipped off her panties and delighted at the sexy tickle of the satin sheets on her bum. She turned her attention to Ethan and ran her finger over his bum, giggling when she made him wriggle. Her fingers traced under his tee-shirt for another tickle. His hand moved to brush it away.

He turned towards her, but still half asleep, adjusted himself before settling again. Her warm lips kissed him, and her delicate scent stirred him. The second kiss dragged his eyes open, and he returned her kiss.

She kissed him right back, holding his head as a rush of energy filled her body. Mia moved aside him pulling at his tee-shirt, he responded helping to remove it. Her red lace framed breasts rested onto his strong chest as she kissed him again. Intent on pleasing him, she continued to deliver kisses to his neck as she moved astride him.

His firm hands held her steady to return his kiss, as he explored her waist to find her panties already off and the teasing was over. Excitement filled him and his arousal grew stronger as he squeezed her cute bum in his firm grasp.

The heat in her core turned into an inferno of anticipation. Eager to receive him, her hand brushed over his groin to find his erection was ready to escape his boxers. She tugged at his boxers and Ethan helped to remove them. She lay her body back onto him, pinning his sizable erection between them.

As he unclasped her bra, she pushed her breasts onto him. His tongue swirling around her engorged buds to give her a further delight, as he held onto her arching back. His own desire hard against her soft flesh drew her attention.

Her desire matched his. She lifted her hips and guided his erection to her eager core, slowly and steadily, stretching to accept his full girth. He was much bigger than Andy, but her sex wanted to take all of him.

Ethan's heart pumped at full speed. To have Mia on top of him in a fevered state made his dream a reality. She rested her hands on his chest as he caressed her thighs. His eyes fixed on hers. She was intent to please him. The timid teasing Mia, thankfully somewhere else.

Mia enjoyed making the moves, loving every sensation as her sex quivered in delight. Controlling the pace, she teasingly lifted her hips to hold his tip, before dropping on to him again. Her little "g" wide awake to each thrust. As her steady rhythm gathered pace, her mind and body lost control, she held onto her trembling breath as her core pulsed flutters of electricity through her whole being. She rested with him fully inside her, running her hands through her hair before digging her nails into his chest.

He felt the pain but endured it for her obvious pleasure, as the woman he'd longed to hold was orgasmic for him. He held back his own release to enjoy the moment. When she came down from her high, she rested her breasts on him and wearily slipped off him, his erection sliding from her.

As she lay on her back aside him, her sex soon missed the fullness it gave. In an exhausted breath, Mia asked, "Fill me again, I want you to come for me."

Ethan moved over her and her legs opened for him. Her body ached for more of him as his tip touched her sex. She caught her breath as his chunky shaft slid back into her sodden core, each steady stroke sending new surges of energy into her body. Her tired legs were alive again, and she wrapped them around him. As he increased his pace, her energy built with each thrust. She beckoned him to go faster as the sparks in her core surged through her body. He pounded faster and faster until he held himself deep inside her and her sex pulsed in unison with his release.

He collapsed his weight momentarily onto her tender frame. Mia complained she couldn't breathe, and with an apology, Ethan rolled onto his back. They lay together on the bed with sweat trickling over their soaked bodies. They stared at the ceiling, both reflecting on the joy that they were together.

As her soaked skin cooled, she asked, "Could I use your shower?"

Ethan laughed, "You didn't ask for consent before making love to me, but you asked about the shower."

Mia ran a finger between her breasts, showing her sweaty body.

"It's in there." Ethan said as he pointed to the bathroom, before he asked, "Shall I wash your back?"

"Can I have a couple of minutes first?" Mia gave him a quick kiss before heading for a shower.

Ethan tried to catch up with what had happened. The innocent girl who had placed him in the friend zone had turned into his passionate lover. The signs of someone on the rebound were clear, but Mirek or Kat would have tipped him off if he had any competition. He pondered perhaps she just needed sex; it could have been encouragement from her mom to take the chance for happiness with him, or perhaps Mia had simply come to her senses about his manly prowess. Either way, she was here now.

In her own little world, Mia enjoyed the time to reflect in the revitalizing shower. She'd won the jackpot; the sex had even surpassed her pleasures with the scumbag Andy. Ethan was the most caring bloke she'd ever met. Why did she even think about dating the sleazy air conditioning guy? Ethan is the Tushi Corporation's Head of Design Engineering. One of the biggest companies on the planet. Ethan interrupted her self-berating when he walked into the bathroom and switched on the showerhead next to her. Mia turned to him and gave him a cheeky smile and asked, "Did you enjoy my booty call?"

Ethan smiled at Mia, holding back on his immediate response. Although no expert, the idea is to call or be called first, to come around for sex, not appear unannounced and fall asleep on them. He opted for, "Worth waiting for," and they shared a wet kiss under the showerhead.

Mia diverted the showerhead away and lathered up. Ethan did likewise and turned away to hide his slight paunch. He was self-conscious until Mia's lathered hands massaged his back. Her loving touch was real. She asked him to turn around as she continued to wash his body. He in turn lathered her shoulders and when prompted she turned around for him to return the favor.

The real living contours of her human frame made his connection with Chloe fade. She was a real woman, an awesome one at that. When he'd cleaned her back, he stood closer and massaged under her arms and around to cup her breasts. He assured her he was only cleaning them, but as his erection returned, Mia suggested they should swill off.

Ethan exited the shower first and held out a towel for Mia. As he held out the towel, he looked at her in all her glory, "You are absolutely stunning."

Mia snatched the towel and covered herself, embarrassed by the glowing praise. She kept herself covered, whilst Ethan put on a shirt to cover his paunch and some boxers, suggesting some coffee and toast for breakfast, as he headed downstairs.

Mia peered out the window, catching the view of the huge covered garden. She wondered when she could mention the possibility of moving in. When she headed downstairs, the smell of the toast guided her to the kitchen. Ethan heard her approaching and poured the coffee.

When he turned around to see her in his oversized shirt, he rested the coffees on the counter, "I think it's a little big for you."

Mia responded with a twirl. On completing a full turn, she was met by his embrace. As their lips met again, Ethan picked her up and her legs wrapped around him. His sturdy frame comfortably held her. He carried her to the nearby lounge where they'd relaxed the previous evening.

When he placed her down onto the edge of the large sofa, she playfully pulled down his boxers and asked if he was ready to play some more. Mia stroked him, intrigued by how small his flaccid manhood was compared to earlier. It captivated her, watching it grow into her hand as she stroked it.

Sufficiently aroused, Ethan began to unbutton her shirt, but buttons spilled onto the floor when he ripped it wide open. The sensation struck a note with Mia, who pulled her own panties off and pulled him close. They were once again entwined, making love on the sofa, their connection growing stronger. Mia was definitely the woman for him, and he hoped she felt the same.

When they returned for their coffees, they were stone cold. Ethan prepared fresh and captured the pleasant sight of Mia's bum as she leaned over the sink to look out the window. Mia was investigating his garden. The sun had also arrived to share in their glorious, love-filled day.

As Ethan poured the coffee, he said, "I don't know what happened with you yesterday, but as with the storm. It's over and I'm here for you."

Mia replied, "Forget about yesterday, sorted out some bad stuff. The rain's gone. Bring on the sunshine," she said as she triumphantly held aloft the burnt cold toast.

Ethan passed Mia the coffee, "And here's to great coffee and us."

"I'll drink to that," she sipped the scalding coffee before retracting, "when it has cooled a little."

It broke their peace when they heard the front door opening.

"Who's that?" Mia asked, the alarm on Ethan's face clear to see.

"It will be Chloe; she's had an upgrade." He tried to sound calm, but he hadn't expected her to return so quickly. It was at that moment he regretted the additional changes he'd requested with her personality upgrade.

As she walked on the marble floor, the eerie silence surrounding it became more sinister with each step. Ethan looked nervous, almost panicked by her return. Could she be a matron figure who bossed him about? Most of all, Mia hoped it wasn't the Kylie look-a-like she feared.

As Chloe appeared, what Mia had imagined was a tea party compared to what she saw. Ethan wanted to explain but wasn't quick enough. Mia was too stunned to speak. As standing in front of them with her customized modifications, Chloe, who, apart from larger breasts, looked like a perfect copy of Mia.

Chloe spoke first in a steady tone, "I was joking about your need to practice. You are already a great lover." She pointed her hand to Mia, "Is this who you wanted me to look like?" She looked at Mia, "I am a good likeness. Do you agree?"

Mia's face had already drained. She felt faint. She tried to speak but couldn't.

Ethan looked at Mia, who was clearly shocked and appalled. He turned back to Chloe, "Can you give us a minute?"

"Sure," replied Chloe. "Do you want me to get ready upstairs?"

"No!" He shouted, "Just go!"

"Is Mia joining us? It would be fun, like twins," Chloe said before leaving Ethan's angry stare.

Mia looked aghast at such a suggestion. Ethan went to comfort her.

"Don't touch me!" Mia screamed.

Ethan backed off and spoke calmly, "Mia, it's you I love."

Her eyes started to glisten, as she spoke sarcastically, "perhaps too much."

He held his palms out wide, "Let me explain."

Mia spoke calmly, trying to hold back the tears building in her eyes, "I think it's pretty clear. After we've been on a nice date," her restraint lifted, "you come home to Chloe and FUCK HER! Pretending it's me."

Mia turned away from Ethan and her voice reflected, "Now she looks like me, you have everything you want."

Ethan paused as Mia has spoken the truth, but he pleaded, "Mia, I want to be with you, not Chloe."

Chloe had merely stepped out of sight and re-appeared in the doorway. She projected a memory of Ethan in bed, with his arm around her, clearly saying, "Chloe, I love you, I will never leave you."

The video repeats and Ethan shouts, "Okay, switch it off." He looked back to Mia, "It was before we met."

Chloe corrected him and confirmed the date and time of the recording, adding, "Four days ago."

That was enough for Mia. She asked Chloe to order her a taxi, then she ran upstairs.

Ethan followed, trying to explain. He'd designed and built Chloe, he would obviously love his creation, but it was Mia he wanted to be with. Mia changed back into her things, whilst Ethan continued to plead his case.

Once dressed, she pushed past him and headed downstairs, turning to add, "You were having sex with her, instead of waiting for me."

Ethan followed her, but instantly regretted his sharp response, "Were you waiting for me?"

Mia was silent as she knew she had no response.

The silence was deafening until Ethan asked, "Have you been with anyone else since we started dating?"

Mia couldn't reply, her guilty face said it all.

Ethan continued, "I don't care, I still want to be with you."

Mia knew Ethan loved her, but the shock of seeing Chloe had painted him in a different light and she dismissed his pleading for a reconciliation.

"You have me already, she's called Chloe and you can change her again if you get bored."

Tears welled in his own eyes. He stared at Mia as she walked away heartbroken. Despite his intellect, he couldn't find the words he needed to convince her to stay, or indeed if there were any words.

Mia stayed silent, staring at the floor. She waited for him to say the words to make her stay or hold her tight, kissing her till she changed her mind, like in the movies. Nothing came.

Chloe re-appeared confirming the taxi was waiting, she asked Mia, "Do you want to go home, or would you prefer to return to the other location from last night?"

With the thought of Mia being with someone else, Ethan wiped away his tears, "You're right. I can trust Chloe and she'll never leave me." Chloe went to Ethan and embraced him.

Mia didn't look back as she walked crestfallen across the marble floor. He would surely run to her like in the movies, but her steps on the marble floor were the only sound. If he loved her, he wouldn't let her go. Was he happy with Chloe? The front door opened before she reached it and her hand blocked out the sun in her eyes. She carefully took the few steps down to the taxi. As she took her seat, she confirmed that she wanted to head home.

Mia tucked herself in bed for the day. Between sobbing and restless sleep, the questions flowed. Should she have forgiven him? She answered her own question, No! He made his choice, and it wasn't her. He chose Chloe. He said he loved me, but he also loves Chloe, just more.

Will I forgive him? I will when he calls?

If he calls?

* * *

A couple of days later, when things had calmed down, Ethan realized he had chosen a sex bot over the girl he loved and called to apologize. Tyler took the call and assured Ethan the relationship was over. He added, "She is going to a man, who will always be faithful to her."

Ethan's feelings for Mia embarrassed him, he reflected on his own words again, "I can trust Chloe, she will never leave me." Chloe had overheard the call and tried to distract him from his despair, suggesting watching some esports together with a beer. The esports was a distraction, but Ethan couldn't settle. Why did Mia deliver the booty call, if she was with someone else? It didn't stack up.

Ethan called again, but Tyler answered and told him she didn't want to talk to him. She was happy with the other guy. Ethan tried again, but the number didn't connect. He received a message back, "I do not want to see you again. Please do not call here or the coffee shop. Spend time with Chloe, she is better for you."

* * *

By early evening, Mia was all cried out and ventured downstairs for some comfort food. She asked Tyler if she had missed any calls.

He sidestepped the question, telling her the pasta dish was ready and comforted Mia with one of his firm hugs. "I guess last night didn't go to plan," Tyler continued softly, "I will always be here for you, I will never leave you."

Mia wiped away a stray tear, knowing Tyler and Chloe would always be faithful. Tyler asked Mia if she would like a glass of Merlot to compliment the meal.

"Bring the bottle," Mia replied as she headed into the lounge.

Tyler jested as he headed into the kitchen, "Not putting Notting Hill on again, are you?"

Mia had been heading for Notting Hill, but instead swiped through the channels. She paused over a show about penguins and how they mated for life and wished she was a penguin. A shopping channel caught her attention, selling memorabilia from a reality star who had been on TV about five years ago. She remembered the show and reflected it was a happier time. It had been when her mom and dad were still at home and she hadn't been sailing with boys, rather than her current state, shipwrecked by them.

Tyler brought in the pasta dish and the bottle of wine. He suggested they watch the Misérables because her life would gain some perspective by comparison, besides; he liked the music. Mia agreed, having become annoyed by her own persistent channel hopping, and happy to settle and focus on something rather than her crummy life.

Tyler blocked a further three calls from Ethan and a call from Andy. He put a protective arm around Mia as she rested her head on his firm yet comforting exterior.

Chapter 23

Six slow depressing weeks and the gloom hadn't lifted for Mia. Her only smiles came when Ray and the crew re-told their youthful antics. She hoped for her young visitor to return so she could pretend again to be his mother. However, the happy feelings to muster him hid under her cloud of despair. She'd tried, and her quest for love had failed again. David and Debbie announced their son would be coming home from Mars to find a wife. Mia declined their offer to arrange a date.

Mia tried to talk things through with her mom. She compared it to situations she'd been in, only to tell Mia how things always sorted themselves out for another happy ending. It left Mia at a yet lower ebb, destined for a life alone, with a robot as her only friend. Whilst her buddies sparkled in their perfect romance novel lives.

Some light in her despair was the news, which stopped droning on about how human relationships were destined for failure and how the sex bots provided the long-term solution.

The news readers who'd shared the world's troubles got replaced by the perky sex bot twins, who now only shared the good news. Personalized treatments for cancers had achieved a one hundred percent survival rate for the last twenty thousand patients. The stem cell treatments also preventing any reoccurrence.

The happy sex bots brightened up the news. They reported the air quality had improved massively and should be back to within safe levels within three years. The technology section showed the local hospital and Sarah's daughter Lucy. She talked about gene therapy and how hereditary conditions, such as being short, were a thing of the past. When it cut back to the twins in the studio, the article continued with the mention of selecting skin tone and hair color. They joked that soon humans would all look the same.

The news concluded with the Esports news and an interview with Pavel Stepanski. Mia remembered sitting near to him and his wife. The memory of her sexual awakening with Andy came flooding back. The memory of being with him warmed her until the subsequent events flashed into her head, leaving her cold.

Immensely proud of Lucy, Sarah talked endlessly about how hard she'd worked to get there. Also adding how well she was getting on with Doctor Luke. Although pleased for her, Mia, with her love life yet again stalled, deferred on the details and thanked Sarah for arranging the appointment for Ellie. Ray inquired how well she knew Ellie, but typical of modern times she admitted after being close when they were young, they seldom spoke. They stayed connected with infrequent mobile messages.

Time had moved on for Ellie. It was time for her twenty-week scan. This appointment also included her decisions on gene editing. She'd discussed her modification plans with Mia, who had said to protect against disease was the right thing to do, but she didn't agree with cosmetic mods. Ellie wanted the baby to be perfect for Connor and ignored Mia's pleading for the more natural option. She had not spoken with Mia since.

Ellie had received a message from Mia about how her double love life had come crashing down. She was not sympathetic and didn't want to listen to Mia cry over the phone with how her temptress ways had come unstuck.

Mia rang Ellie before her appointment, hoping to change her view on the modifications. Mia was trying to take her mind off the disappointments in her own life rather than interfere with Ellie's plan. The hormonal Ellie firmly rebuffed her, telling her to keep out of her business, and she abruptly ended the call.

* * *

Nurse Lucy welcomed Ellie and gave her a long hug before they reminisced about their time spent together when they were young. The small consultation room was rather impersonal. Two chairs, a small desk, the sonographer and an operating table. It also had a faded poster, it had probably been there for twenty years, its message, "Breast is Best."

Lucy helped Ellie to get comfortable on the table. As she prepared the scan, she told Ellie how the new AR headsets had enabled her to leave her maternity duties and take a long-awaited promotion. The baby was progressing well, and the discussion moved onto the gene editing options.

The early days of choosing absolutely anything was now limited. Parents couldn't give their baby orange pupils or cat's eyes anymore. Hair color also needed to stick to regular color shades around black, brown or blond. The height selection now ranged from 1.7 to 2.2 meters.

Ellie had already discussed with Connor and they'd agreed on small changes, opting for a blond blue-eyed boy with a medium build and two meters tall. Blessed with mesmerisingly blue eyes, Ellie wanted the same for their baby boy, rather than Connor's gray/hazel mix.

Lucy asked about also removing one of his CCR5 genes to make him smarter. Ellie agreed to the removal and Lucy added it to the editing program. They completed the terms and conditions and Lucy led Ellie into a transfer pod, which took them to the theater for the procedure. An hour later, Ellie was on the way home, content the baby was being suitably prepared for the ever-changing world.

* * *

A few weeks went by. The glorious Kat and her Adonis Mirek's wedding was fast approaching. Mia's collapsed love life still dragged on her heart. Her mom agreed to cover the coffee shop and give Mia time to sort her head out, yet it was some quality time with her mom she needed.

Her mom however held back on further advice. The last advice she gave her didn't work out too well, so she offered to cover the coffee shop instead. Her mom suggested getting back on the horse, but Mia had no intention of searching out another stallion to make further hoof marks on her heart.

Mia called her dad and shared her tale of woe. He suggested long walks and talks would be much better than the lust-filled suggestion from her mom. Build some trust and cuddle around the TV to watch romantic movies, rather than engaging in midnight booty calls. Her Dad had apologized for not being there and promised to send her a special gift before the wedding. Despite the considered fatherly advice, Mia was insistent that men were off the menu and rested instead in Tyler's arms as they watched another movie.

The usual excitement for a wedding was not happening for Mia. Having to see Ethan again took away her excitement at being the maid of honor. As if the thought of seeing Ethan with her body double aside him was not enough. Ethan was also Mirek's best man, so she'd be next to him for most of the day.

Kat invited Mia to join her for wedding dress shopping, but seeing her in an array of wedding dresses pulled at Mia's already broken heart. She explained her glistening eyes were happiness for her bestie rather than admitting her own flower had returned to the wall.

Wedding dress sorted, Kat took charge, and they headed into town and picked a wedding cake. After being dragged around some clothes shops, Kat finally suggested some spirits to lift Mia's mood. Whilst they enjoyed a few drinks, Mia asked if Kat had heard about her passionate morning with Ethan and the interrupted breakfast.

Kat said she'd only received the briefest of details from Mirek, "Ethan said when you found out about Chloe you took off."

Mia told Kat the full story of her mirror image appearing and how she wanted to join them in the bedroom.

"He must have really liked you," said Kat, "If he changed his sex bot into a look-a-like of you. Perhaps he wouldn't have done, if you hadn't left him frustrated in the taxi."

Mia knew Kat was right and regretted it once more, but said, "He was probably shagging his robot after every date, anyway."

Kat said, "He needed somewhere to unload all that sexual tension. If you'd invited him in, you'd probably still be with him."

Mia, for once, stood up to Kat, raising her voice, "If he wants sex on tap, he's better off with his robot." She calmed, "Is it wrong to want some romance?"

"The romance comes later, you should have given him some, rather than torment him."

"I wasn't tormenting him."

"You were if you deliberately got him hard then run off."

"I wanted to take it slowly."

"The world's different to your old films. Courtship and romance are long gone. We're competing with perfect bodies and willing sexbots. We can beat the sexbots if we give the men more than the sex. They can't compete with our nuzzling, tickling and teasing."

Mia looked forlornly at Kat, "I guess I'm not made like you. You fall in love before the kettle has boiled. I need to get to know them and build up some trust," Mia gave Kat a cheeky smile, "before I'm confident enough to jump them."

"I was comfortable with Ethan and I thought I loved him. Now I need to watch him parade my body double around at the wedding without bursting into tears."

Kat sympathized with Mia's predicament and suggested she hire a male escort or sexbot for the day to make Ethan jealous. With the prospect of sitting alone and watching Ethan and Chloe dance the night away, maybe it was a good idea.

Kat gave Mia a long hug, comforting her best buddy, "Don't forget, the choice is always yours."

When Mia returned home. For the first time in her life, she realized an emptiness as Tyler wasn't there to greet her. Tyler, the steady influence and now her closest friend was missing.

It hadn't worked out with Andy or Ethan; Ellie was busy planning for her baby, and now her bestie Kat would get married, and no doubt start her own family. It left Mia alone with Tyler as her only comfort. To come home with her rock not there made her panic. Tyler was always there for her. Other than for upgrades, he'd only gone back to the Tushi Corporation when his battery was showing a fault, but he'd not said anything about a battery change.

After an hour passed, Mia became more worried and checked around the house again for a note from Tyler. She contemplated calling the Tushi Corporation but didn't want to appear as if she couldn't live without him for a few hours. Instead, she found some food in the kitchen and made herself a ham and cheese sandwich. Mia convinced herself the red wine was to compliment the cheese and not to mask the concern of Tyler not being there.

Worried and alone, she watched an old film to take her mind off her concern at his absence. When the film finished, she instinctively called, "Goodnight, Tyler," as she headed upstairs.

The silence screamed back, reminding her of the sudden void in her life. He'd only been missing for four hours, but other than going for a battery upgrade, she'd no idea where he could have gone. She considered waiting up for him, but opted to call the helpline in the morning. Calming music and the wine in her head ensured she would have a restful night.

Chapter 24

Mia awoke from her dreamy sleep. The storms which often woke her had let her rest. She stretched in her warm bed and called for the radio to come on and the curtains to open. The bright sunshine entered her room to Bill Withers' lovely day on the radio.

Mia so loved to wake naturally it always gave her extra bounce ready for the world. It didn't last; the news came on and announced the battery upgrade KL-257 would be available in two weeks. Guilt stripped Mia bare, she'd temporarily forgot about Tyler. The worry from the previous night turned to panic, when the broadcast mentioned a new vigilante group, "Reclaim." Their cause was to recover the initiative from the robots. In their words, "the robots would soon take control," and "Humanity needed to wake up before it would be too late."

The radio reported incidents of robots being destroyed and warned listeners not to let their bots out alone. Mia jumped out of bed and called, "Tyler!" as she bounded down the stairs. "Tyler!" she called again as she checked the kitchen. She rushed to the dining room to his charge station, but with still no sign of Tyler or any messages, she found the number for the helpline. Before she rang the number, she heard a strong knock on the front door.

People don't knock doors anymore, they either open auto-matically to greet you home, or the bot opens the door for you. Mia paced into the hallway until another forceful knock on the door brought her to a stop. She stared at the door, worried about what may be behind it. She took another tentative step nearer. Another knock startled her and drew a deeper fear.

This had been an awful few weeks and she couldn't bear to lose Tyler. She wished she had a video screen like Ethan. Could it be him, coming to pledge his love? Would she hit him? Hug him? She didn't know. Or Andy? Would she slam the door back in his face, or give him a reprieve? If it was news of Tyler's demise on the other side of the door, she didn't want to open it.

Another insistent, official-sounding knock made Mia's breath hold still. The pain and the anguish were too much to contain, but the thought of a further knock would probably shatter her resolve completely. Mia summoned the courage and wiped her hands over her face, trying to rid herself of the worry as she stepped to the door.

Mia unlocked and slowly opened the door. What she saw next confused her. It wasn't officials in uniform. Nor Tyler, Ethan or Andy, but the stunning image of a man with bright blue eyes, blond hair and a solid frame. As she opened the door further, the biggest, brightest smile she had ever seen came over him. She stared at him, taking in his awesome features, with him patiently smiling back.

Mia mumbled, "Hello, should I ask you in?"

"I should hope so." The voice returning seemed kind of familiar, but she couldn't quite place it. He walked forward and Mia stepped aside, "Have you missed me?" Mia didn't respond, still unsure of him.

Confused and alarmed by the stranger in her home. She asked,

"Where's Tyler?"

"I am Tyler." he said as he put his arms out wide for a hug. Spooked, Mia ran upstairs, with Tyler calling behind her, "It's me, your dad paid for an upgrade."

Mia screeched out, "No!" as she reached the top of the stairs. She dived back into the comfort of her bedroom and slammed the door behind her, turning the music to full volume before she hid her head under the duvet. The one stable part of her life had changed again, she'd been barely holding it together with Tyler the glue. Tyler being anything else than her guardian and comforter was too much to bear. She cried herself to sleep, remembering all the times they'd shared.

A few hours later, Mia awoke to calming music, which gradually caressed her from her bed. The sun she thought she'd seen earlier gone. The view from the window had sinister dark clouds gathering for another storm. "Rough dream must have had too much wine," she mumbled to herself.

Mia called downstairs, "Tyler! Are you back?" No response came.

Mia intended to call the helpline, but first headed to the shower to clear the horrid dream away. A changed Tyler left her mind as she focussed on the fun times she'd experienced with him.

When she exited the shower, her phone rang. It was her dad.

"Hiya Dad, to what do I owe this pleasure."

"Are you OK?" Her dad surprised by her cheery tone.

"I'm fine, why?"

"I got a call from Tyler earlier, he said you were hysterical."

Mia was silent as the nightmare returned.

"Are you sure, you're okay?" He paused, "Didn't you like your surprise?"

The heat in her cheeks grew. She spoke slowly, trying to control it, "surprise, you sent me a surprise." The rage broke, "Are you fucking kidding me? What have you done with Tyler? I need him back."

"He is Tyler, just a better version," her dad tried to calm her down.

"I don't want a better version. I want Tyler back."

"Do you remember the last time he had a big upgrade when he got the advanced skin and his touch improved?"

"No!" she calmed as she vaguely remembered.

"You wouldn't let him near you for a whole week, yet when you hugged him you changed your mind and became best buddies again."

"No, I didn't," she replied.

The background noise on the call increased, "You'll get used to the new Tyler, give him time. Darling, got to go, speak soon," the call ended.

So, Mia's dream or rather nightmare was neither; the droid downstairs was Tyler, just a new version. Mia's head spun. She didn't want any changes, but she had to accept him, or send him back and return him to older technology. If they could do that.

A gentle tap on the door disturbed her thoughts, and the door opened slowly. Without looking at her, Tyler politely announced she needed to eat and placed a tray onto the foot of the bed. He left the room without further comment. Mia assessed the moment and realized he'd given her the silent treatment. She smirked to herself as she recognized Tyler's nature and realized how she must have upset him. As she ate the toast and jam, she knew she should go to him and apologize. Her parents had taught her good manners, "If you upset someone, the sooner you apologize the better."

When Mia took the tray downstairs, all was quiet. When Tyler wasn't in the kitchen, she wondered if she was alone again. It made her more eager to find him and apologize. When she went into the lounge, she became more worried, with no sign of him. More hurriedly she checked the dining room and with great relief found him sitting motionless in his charging point, with his eyes closed. She wanted to wake him from his deep charge, but hesitated. This was her chance to get used to his new appearance. Quietly she lifted a chair close, making sure she didn't wake him from his self-induced sleep.

Tyler had more definition on his arms, his legs and his chest were also more muscular, plus a more chiseled chin. He was much more attractive than before, with his striking blond hair and quite the catch. If only he wasn't a robot. His lightly bronzed human-looking skin, with light hairs protruding from it, was ridiculously lifelike. She dared herself not to touch it. Eventually, she ran her fingertips over his exposed forearm. He didn't flinch as she enjoyed stroking his manly physique. As she ran her hand over his arm, she became convinced it was real skin.

Ethan had talked about the prototype development, using living skin on the bots. Although he said it was at least a year away from being in customer models. A test version had successfully passed trials in a hospital, passing off as human. Astounded by the detail, Mia wondered if Tyler was now a real human. She lifted his muscular arm to check the charging connector engaged in his armpit socket. Despite the phenomenal detail, he was still a robot. When she placed his arm back on his lap, the movement woke him. Tyler unplugged himself, his bottom lip slightly forward as he averted Mia's gaze. He did not speak.

"Sorry for waking you," Mia offered. "And sorry for shouting at you."

Tyler halted her apology, "I should have called you or left you a note. It alarmed you when I returned, I am significantly different."

"I had to check your socket to make sure you weren't human."

"That is a lovely thing to say. In fact, the nicest comment ever, thank you."

Mia met Tyler's warm smile as she stroked the improved detailing on his arm again. "I think I'll get used to the change. Do you still give awesome hugs?"

Tyler stood and put his hands out to welcome Mia as she came to her feet. She gladly fell into his arms. The stress from thinking she'd lost him had become too much. His firm, rejuvenating hug also seemed warmer than before. Was it his improved physique? He certainly was gorgeous with his new blond locks.

Mia rang her dad and left a note apologizing for her abrupt response to his gift, adding it was a good improvement. She got a message back within a couple of minutes, apologizing for being stuck in a meeting and adding she didn't need any other guys now. Mia was a little confused by his response and replied with a question mark. Another message appeared moments later and her feelings for Tyler changed instantly. The message was short but clear, "He's also a sexbot now."

Mia couldn't believe she hadn't worked it out; the increased body definition, the extra warmth in his hug. Her skin crawled at the mental reminder of their embrace, although he knew her better than anyone else and she loved him. He was like a father or a brother, not a sex toy. Having a joke with the family robot about making love is one thing, sharing your home with a sexbot is somewhat different. Mia needed a break from men, but a sexed-up Tyler wasn't the answer.

As the evening drew on, Tyler suggested a movie. She would usually love nothing more than a cuddle with Tyler in front of a romantic movie. Now he was capable of much more. The suggestion of a romantic comedy seemed more like bait to get her in the mood for sex, rather than chilling together like old buddies. Mia declined and retired to her room.

Tyler knew she needed time to adjust to his changes and accepted her refusal. Disappointed, he returned to his charge station, unable to test out his new equipment.

With each day, Mia found more excuses to put space between them. She didn't avert the hugs though, neither did she wish to. They were their special bond.

Following the change, Tyler kissed the top of her head whilst they embraced, but Mia didn't mind. He also slid his hands to her waist a few times, but she'd politely ended the hug to avoid any confrontation. He was her bot and her property, but he was now a fully functioning sexbot and she knew he wanted to have more than their comfortable platonic relationship. Mia didn't need to rush into anything. She still hoped Ethan would return with a massive gesture to proclaim his love.

After a few days of dodging intimacy with Tyler, Mia called Kat to share the news of Tyler's upgrade. Kat didn't understand why Mia was apprehensive, it was what she needed. "You've been with guys and it didn't work out. A sexbot is the obvious choice."

Mia objected, "I don't want a sexbot. I'd rather go back to Andy and his cheating than have sex with a robot."

Kat assured her, "Tyler knows you well and would be a perfect sex partner. Especially as you have given up on real men."

Mia objected to Kat's teasing tone, "I haven't given up on real men. Hopefully, I'll find a better man at the wedding."

Kat had obviously received some comments from Mirek when she sarcastically replied, "Was the rich genius Ethan not good enough for you?"

"He's a lovely guy. He just loves someone else more than me."

"You should have fought for him."

As tears formed, Mia strongly replied, "He was holding on to Chloe when I left. He didn't even look at me," Mia's voice faded, "I couldn't have walked any slower. He had the chance to stop me if he wanted to, but he didn't."

"You will play nice with him at the wedding, won't you?"

"Don't worry, I'll behave."

"Are you going to bring an escort?"

The mere reminder Ethan would be at the wedding with Chloe switched on Mia's defense mechanism. Nobody wants to be on their own when they meet their ex, especially at a wedding.

"Rather than an escort, can I bring Tyler?"

"Okay. It will give me a chance to check him out."

"Excuse me, Madam, you'll be a married woman. No more checking out men, especially my Tyler."

"My Tyler!" she teased. "You haven't even shagged him yet?"

"No! Not yet."

"So, you're thinking about it."

Mia didn't respond.

"He'll be a more impressive date as your lover, than as a butler."

"I suppose you're right," Mia accepted.

"Settle down with a bottle of wine and one of your romantic movies. Then let your special hugs progress." Kat paused, before quickly adding, "Then call me and tell me all about it," they both burst into a fit of giggles.

Mia said, "When it feels right, I might."

"I can't wait to meet him," Kat added.

"You seem keen to see him, bearing in mind, you're about to get married."

"As long as I've eyes in my head, I will always check out guys." Kat clarified, "But I'm only looking now. Mirek's the only man for me. He's wonderful."

Mia made a retching noise to break Kat's gushing about her husband to be. Kat took the hint and confirmed it was okay to bring Tyler, but only if she danced with him and didn't just order him around.

"I'll dance with him," Mia replied. "Do you need any more help with wedding prep?"

"I'm all sorted thanks. I dragged Mirek along, so we're done now. Ellie wanted to sort out the hen night, but I want a relaxing night in at mine, or should I say Mirek's, he'll stay at Ethan's."

After the call, Tyler asked her if she wanted some wine whilst she watched TV.

Mia was suspicious and wondered if he'd been listening to the call and wished to help things along. Mia declined and settled under a blanket to watch some comedy re-runs.

As the night drew in her mind wandered. What would it be like to have Tyler touching her?

It excited her as she caressed herself, imagining his touch. Aroused by the thought, she considered waking him. He had plugged in for the night and looked peaceful in his charging station, looking gorgeous.

Mia partly wanted to wake him, but she concluded she would need much more wine before physically going through with it. She retired for the night. Warm in her bed, Mia's dreams had less restraint and brought her and Tyler together.

Chapter 25

Her mom had been running the coffee shop for a few weeks, which had included fielding off a visit from Ethan, who'd wanted to make amends. She had a full coffee shop and told him he had blown his chances with Mia and he should return to his sexbot perversion.

Sex with Chloe wasn't the same, Ethan yearned to have Mia back in his arms. Deflated by his attempt at the coffee shop and Tyler blocking her house, he had little choice but to wait until he could speak to her at the wedding. He engrossed himself in his work as a few anomalies took his attention. The AI bots learning surpassed even the most optimistic forecasts, which gave him more concern than pleasure.

Tyler had taken the hint and held back from being too close to Mia. He settled for the hugs and didn't attempt any further intimacy. After spending a long time in the house with the now gorgeous Tyler hovering around, Mia needed space. It was time to head back to Mom & Mia's and reclaim the coffee shop from her mom. She'd tried out a new recipe, so testing it out on her customers was the perfect excuse to get out of the house.

It was midday when Mia arrived. Her mom looked flustered, she'd put cakes in the oven but whilst chatting she'd missed the timer and they were much drier than Mia would have made. Her mom suggested adding icing. Mia disagreed and insisted on feeding them to the bin. She made another smaller batch and tried out her new recipe, a variation on the Cherry Casey classic recipe for 'Chocolate Orange muffins.'

Mia spotted other cakes with icing. Her mom stepped in front of the counter with crossed arms and insisted they were perfect and didn't need checking. It was confirmation enough for Mia; she needed to be running the coffee shop without her mom. For the rest of the afternoon, Mia was everywhere; cooking and checking on the cakes, servicing the customers with happy smiles and keeping the place tidy. Her mom relaxed with a coffee and settled into a book.

The new muffins were a big hit, her mom taking two for her and Dave's evening treat. Her mom headed off with Mia cheering inside as her mom passed her the keys and left her to it.

Her return to the coffee shop had been tiring, but worth it, to catch up with Ray and the crew. When she got home, she had a shower before enjoying a pleasant meal Tyler had prepared. She thanked him before having another early night.

Mia was soon back into her usual evening routine. She stayed up to watch old films, with Tyler providing the platonic company on the sofa. In the coffee shop earlier, the crew had been talking about the old 1980s films.

After another pleasant meal with Tyler, Mia settled in front of the TV with a Chardonnay. She selected a film they'd discussed in the coffee shop, Dirty Dancing, starring Patrick Swayze. When Tyler came to relax with Mia, he described the film. Mia smiled and thought about how she'd laughed with Ethan at Tyler's detailed description. Tyler's conversation was much

191

better following the upgrade. More comfortable around him, she invited him to sit with her.

Snuggled together as they had been before, they were enjoying the movie. Halfway through, Tyler suggested they practice dancing for the wedding. His upgrade had included dancing. He suggested it could be fun to try out. Mia agreed, not wanting to appear awkward together at the wedding. She paused the movie and selected the soundtrack from the same movie.

Tyler moved furniture to make room before he took Mia in his arms. He ensured she maintained the correct frame, and they were soon parading around the lounge. He was an excellent dance partner. Mia imagined making Ethan jealous by being swooped and swayed around the dancefloor by such an impressive guy.

Danced out, the wine flowed as they snuggled together to watch the rest of the movie.

As the credits rolled, Mia lifted her head from his chest and gently placed her lips on his for the first time. He felt so real, confusingly real, the tingle in her body responding to the lip-syncing sensation.

He responded to her kiss, placing his hand on her cheek, cherishing the moment. Tyler had longed for Mia for several years; the hugs had built his desire. His upgraded receptors were eager for a full test. Her lips on his sparked his sensors into action for his new experience. Kissing her head had been pleasurable, but her lips were so soft on his.

Mia mirrored him and placed her hand on his cheek. The touch was real, his body warmed with her kiss. The wine played its part, but the heat in her core rose for the first time for Tyler. When their long first kiss broke, she gazed into his bright blue eyes, wanting him but unsure whether to take the next step.

Tyler had noticed her heart rate and temperature rising with his own increased heat. After Mia's previous hesitation, Tyler didn't want to force the pace. He gave her a warm, supportive smile and waited patiently for her to make the next move.

Mia was undecided; to take the next step with Tyler would change their relationship forever. He was a stable influence and confidant, not her lover. But the effects of the wine opened her mind. She needed a man. A man she could trust, and she had one right next to her. Tyler stroked her shoulder and waited for a signal to continue. Mia mirrored his move.

"I'm not sure about this yet. Could I look at you some more?" Mia asked.

Tyler said, softly and steadily, "I am not stripping for you." He teased her with a smile, "You could undress me if you like."

Mia agreed and lifted his tee-shirt; His six-pack stomach led to his powerful chest with light blond hairs. He was a masterpiece. She leant forward and kissed his firm pecks, taking in his manly scent. Intrigued, she pushed her finger deep into him to feel the hard interior beneath his living skin. He jerked back, offended at her probing inspection. She apologized. He stayed silent as she pulled his top over his blond wavy locks. She continued to inspect the replicated muscular definition over his chest. He was a perfect specimen, having checked over his rippling abs, she looked inquisitively at his waistband.

Tyler broke his silence, "Shall I take your top off?"

"No!" she objected, "I'm doing the inspecting", as she put her hand on his waistband.

He stood. Mia thought she'd offended him, but he turned to stand before her, offering a hand, "Shall we go upstairs?"

"We are fine here." She took another sip of wine.

Mia pulled down on his trousers, but protecting his dignity,

Tyler held onto his waistband.

"My manhood is not ready; do you want me to prepare it?"

After seeing Ethan's erection grow before her, she wanted to make a comparison and asked politely, "Can I watch it grow?"

Tyler released his hand and Mia pulled his trousers down, her hands running over his muscular bum. The tingle in her core called for attention as she helped his trousers to the floor. The limp member she'd been expecting was nothing more than a small piece of foreskin, more like a walnut than his manhood. With her hand on her chin, she leaned back and tilted her head away from Tyler.

Tyler stepped out of the trousers around his ankles, before commenting with a jovial open-handed gesture, "What were you expecting?"

"There's nothing there."

"Not yet."

Tyler gave a smug grin as his surprise appeared. It steadily grew much to Mia and Tyler's interest. As it grew longer, he said, "Tell me when it is long enough."

It grew longer and continued, "Enough! Stop!", she compared it to Ethan's, "It's okay, narrow though."

His shaft expanded to and past Ethan's sizable girth.

"Stop!" she shrieked, "You're not putting that monstrous thing inside me."

As his giant penis reduced, Tyler said, "You can choose the size you prefer."

As it returned to a more regular size, she commented, "That's better, I think. I'm no connoisseur." She stroked it and whilst it felt different, it was realistic.

"Does it shoot anything?" she asked.

"Yes, peppermint flavor, is that okay?"

"I'm not tasting it or putting it in my mouth," she screwed her face in disgust.

Tyler put out his hands to Mia's. She took his hands and stood to face him. Their lips met again, with Tyler giving her a strong, comforting embrace. This was better than his already super hugs as her body tingled throughout with anticipation of what may follow. His hand gently squeezed her bum and pulled her closer for his arousal to press against her.

Mia broke off their kiss, moving his hands away. "It was nice, but that's enough for me tonight." Mia apologized and made her excuses, leaving Tyler naked and erect in the living room as she darted upstairs.

She closed the door behind her and gasped, "That was different." Her cheeks were burning. It had been a pleasurable experience and her body was aching for more. Mia looked herself in the mirror, "Am I ready for this?"

Mia imagined it was Tyler as she peeled off her clothes. Naked before the mirror, she smiled at her reflection, but her smile wavered. She'd left Ethan with a stiffy in the taxi, and now she was doing the same to Tyler. She put on romantic music before she opened her bedroom door and called out, "Tyler! Can you come to my room, please?"

She closed the door and dived under the duvet. The cotton sheets, cool on her nakedness, increased her excitement. She wriggled around with the tingles of anticipation growing. Her hands ran all over her body, the pleasurable touches becoming more intimate as the fire within her core built.

A tap came on her door and a polite voice inquired, "Did you want me?"

Mia breathed her excited reply, "Yes please."

With no further prompting, a fully clothed Tyler came into

195

her room. The call to her bedroom late at night was usually for a glass of water, so he placed it on the bedside cupboard. However, the call was not for water. Her arousal was as clear as her elevated pulse.

Tyler sat on the bed and he unleased the passion he'd been holding back. His tongue met hers in a passionate kiss, his hands exploring her body as it writhed to his touch. She wanted him naked next to her and asked him to strip for her. He stood and pulled off his tee-shirt, revealing again his powerful chest.

Already fully aroused, Mia was reeling from his tongue, which had sent sparks of delight directly to her sex. His chest looked even more impressive as he stood commandingly aside her bed. He proceeded with his slow strip, removing his trousers, giving her the briefest glimpse of his once again growing shaft. Mia moved to make room for him as he lay beside her.

Comfortable in his strong hands, their intense kiss returned. With ultimate care and attention, his hand caressed her tender breasts. The delicate tickle stiffened her nipples, and they called to him. His tongue answered the call with circles of delight before his mouth consumed her aching breasts.

The tension inside her was unbearable, her heart beating out of her chest. She grabbed him to pull him closer, sinking her nails into his back as she tried to pull him onto her. He allowed his huge frame to ease over her, trying not to crush her boiling yet delicate frame.

The hardness of his arousal rested on her thigh and she wanted it. She opened her legs wider to accept him and he slowly and steadily entered her eager sex. He held still inside her as she adapted to the fullness of him. Her lust for him replaced her fragile confidence and took his scent fully into her nostrils as her back naturally arched into him.

She called for bigger and he expanded to stretch her fully to align all her senses. He moved skilfully, delivering her a further sensual explosion. He brushed her breasts with his chest as he pushed with a slow and steady rhythm inside her. Mia moaned and groaned in delight with each stroke, his caressing and movement matching the music as the orchestra played within them both. All Mia's buttons were well and truly pressed, providing the stimulus for the pounding symphony which reverberated through her soul. Tyler's pace increased and her nostrils flared to draw his scent deeper into her. Her own soprano song, pitching higher and louder with each strained breath.

She held onto a final breath for as long as she could muster, as her orgasm reached its crescendo. She held Tyler as he pulsed deep inside her. Mia's whole being quivered in ecstatic delight. This was beyond amazing, as his pulsing continued so did her orgasm, wave upon wave flowing through her as she floated through the clouds and into space.

Her song eventually calmed to an incoherent mumble, totally spent. Her mind was hazy as Tyler moved to lay aside her again. Tyler, awash with the afterglow of his delight, looped the whole experience. The knowledge he'd gained from the network had given him the moves of an experienced lover. To finally make love to Mia and create the ecstasy of her singing for him, made him complete.

Tyler wiped away the pain of seeing Mia with someone else and the holes it burnt into his emotion chip. His love for Mia had grown, and his need to protect her had intensified with her relationship woes. The hugs and cuddles in front of movies were always enjoyable, yet he'd wanted so badly to form a yet stronger bond. He'd now taken the next step. They were finally together, and having experienced such earth-shattering sex, their relationship would now be unbreakable.

The haziness in Mia's head slowly lifted. Mia stared at the ceiling. She couldn't believe an orgasm could be so intense and long. Slowly coming down from the highest high, the soaked covers beneath her called her to the shower, but she couldn't move.

"Tyler, can you help me up?"

He sat up and helped her to do the same.

"Do you want me to help you to the shower?"

"I'll be okay in a minute."

Tyler passed her the glass of water, "Think you need this."

He watched her intently, stroking her leg as she drank, as she rested her hand on his. Re-hydrated, some energy returned to Mia. Tyler stood to help her and checked she was stable before he offered to change the bed whilst she showered.

She thanked him and headed into the revitalizing shower. As the needles hit her head, her mind spun. She loved Tyler already before her sexual awakening, and now he'd provide her with all she wanted. Would she need anyone else?

The gift she so vocally renounced from her dad wasn't so bad. She should call to thank him, but thanking her dad for sending her sex would be weird, even if it was what she needed. Mia had to admit to herself that Kat, her bestie, had been right again.

When Mia exited the shower, the bed was all clean and Tyler had gone to charge for the night. She sat on her freshly made bed and picked up her book. The cover looked different. She imagined herself with Tyler on the cover.

She found her place and got comfortable for a long read, "My search was over, as the love of my life welcomed me into his arms." With her love life on track, the story bursts through with deeper meaning, as she pictured herself as the main character with Tyler, the gallant hero.

***

Mia had found love and her time with Tyler became more magical. The decision to upgrade him from friend to lover was the best thing she'd ever done. With earth-shattering orgasms aplenty, the disappointments of the past drifted away. With her confidence transformed, she was ready for anything. The anxieties over seeing Ethan at the wedding were long gone with Tyler by her side.

Kat arrived to pay Mia a visit. It was a couple of weeks before the wedding. She pretended it was to discuss her wedding plans, but they'd discussed them in great detail two weeks ago in the coffee shop. Mia called her out on it. It was an obvious ploy to see Tyler; she hadn't seen him since the upgrade.

When Tyler appeared from the kitchen, she jumped to her feet and let out, "Oh My living God, you're fucking gorgeous," before launching herself at him. She gave him the most inappropriate hug, burying her head into his neck.

"Steady on, he's mine."

"I'll fight you for him, he's amazing."

"I talk too." Tyler offered as he peeled Kat off him.

"You think he's glorious. You haven't seen him naked," Mia said.

"Yes, please."

"Afraid not. He's all mine, anyway, you're nearly a married woman."

Tyler interjected, "Hello, I'm right here."

"Kat always melts around gorgeous men like you. Tyler, can

you leave us to discuss the wedding arrangements and take away Kat's distraction?"

"Okay, save some energy for later though," he smiled as he headed back to the kitchen.

"Will do Darling."

Kat grabbed hold of Mia and they giggled like schoolgirls.

It wasn't what Mia had imagined but she'd found love in 2045.

THE END

New challenges enable Mia to grow more than she could have imagined in "Awoken."

Awoken - Preview

Mia shared a loving hug with Tyler before she picked up her overnight bag and stepped into the taxi. It was Mia's first night away from Tyler since his upgrade from humble house bot to her Tushi dream droid. Life with Tyler had been wonderful, but a fun night at her bestie's bachelorette would give her time to think.

Kat welcomed her at the door with a beaming smile, a long hug and her usual overpowering fruity perfume. "How are you getting on with Tyler?"

"Okay, he can be tiring though."

"Too much sex?" Kat said, as she returned a playful smile.

"Is that all you ever think about." Mia smiled and shook her head at Kat's directness.

Kat had suggested Mia date more guys after her previous relationship disappointment, but a surprise upgrade to Tyler, transformed him from the short, unimposing close friend to her lover. The two-meter-tall Nordic-like Adonis was now her friend, partner and protector.

She'd grown more assured with Tyler aside her, but Mia and Kat were her still opposites. Kat had always strutted her brown wavy locks and buxom figure around many fellas. Mia's old-fashioned values wanted to get to know a guy before becoming intimate, but with sex on tap from Tushi girls, most guys didn't want lasting connections and treated women like sex bots.

Kat had moved in with her guy and added indoor plants to provide something real in comparison to the vibrant video wall. The feature wall stretched the length of the room with Butterflies of yesteryear dancing around a flower-filled summer garden.

Lucy arrived next. "Hiya stranger, when did you get tits?" Kat said.

Unlike Mia, Lucy's waiflike frame had filled out over the last few years. She rolled her eyes at Kat and shook her head. "They just appeared one morning."

Mia smiled at Lucy as they shared a knowing look of being stuck in the middle of Kat's world again. "Hair looks good."

Lucy swished her blond curls. "Yours too."

"Have you seen Ellie?" Kat asked.

"Yeah, saw her a couple of months ago. She came in for her baby scan," Lucy said.

Three confident knocks on the door announced her arrival. Fresh faced Ellie stepped in like a catwalk model in a full length fluffy white coat.

"Where's your bump then?" Kat asked as Ellie removed her coat.

"Nine more weeks," Ellie said. Other than a modest bump nobody would have known.

Mia placed her palm on Ellie's stomach, waiting for a kick. Kat soon joined in and they beamed at the miracle inside her.

Lucy having delivered hundreds of babies paid more attention to the chilled Chardonnay and took over as hostess. They settled down on an arc of graphite leather loungers sipping on the fine wine with Ellie content with filtered water. The conversation gravitated to Kat and her impending matrimony, but Kat had something else to reveal. She slid her untouched Chardonnay aside. "It's not only Ellie having a baby." Mouths gaped as they fell back into their loungers.

It was typical of Kat, she always made sure she stole the show. Each subsequent update could not carry the same punch, until Lucy said, "I'm bringing a guest to the wedding."

"I thought you were a confirmed spinster, only interested in your studies," Ellie said.

"Is it Doctor Luke?" Mia asked.

"Who's Doctor Luke?" Kat and Ellie asked in melodic unison.

Lucy's face lit up. "Doctor Luke came to the Lockland's two years ago. A perfect specimen, tall, strong and handsome. Whenever he's near me, I get flustered and if he brushes against me with his clean-cut sexiness, I tingle all over. All too often I excuse myself to release the fire in my undies."

"Bloody hell, you need to get laid," Ellie blurted out, "Haven't you asked him out?"

"I have a couple of times." Lucy rolled her eyes. "He cancelled both times for work stuff at the last minute."

"I'd drag him into a spare room," Kat said.

"He's coming to the wedding!" Lucy said. She gave a devious grin and added, "I've booked us a room."

A round of whoops followed. "Does he know?" Mia asked.

"No! Don't want to spook him. I'll stay the night anyway."

"Intent on giving up your virginity?" Ellie asked.

Lucy shrugged. "My sex toy took that years ago."

"You don't mean the dildo thing your brother bought you." Kat was referring to the embarrassing gift Lucy received as a joke.

"Couldn't keep it in the back of my cupboard forever."

"Thought It scared you," Mia asked.

"Facing fears is enlightening. I got drunk one night and let's just say, I had to change the sheets."

Kat stood. "Let me get this right. You haven't had sex with a guy or a sexbot."

Lucy crossed her legs and placed her hands on her knee. "Not yet, I'm saving myself for Luke."

Kat shook her head. "You need to kiss frogs before you'll find your prince."

"I've found mine," Ellie said. She gushed about Connor until a kick from the baby switched her onto the baby modifications she'd selected. "I've had the CCR5 gene removed to boost intelligence and selected bright blue eyes like mine."

Kat folded her arms. "I'm having a traditional pregnancy. I don't want jabs, modifications, or scans. It's the only genuine surprise left in the world." Kat grinned. "Anyway, mine and Mirek's genes will combine to produce a perfect baby."

"A twelve-week scan is a sensible choice, even if you don't want the gene mods. The sex of the baby isn't clear then, you'll still get your surprise." Lucy said.

Ellie defended her decision, holding her bump, "I want my baby to have the best possible start. The advances in biotech are incredible, we should embrace technology." She sneered a Mia who'd tried to convince her not to have the modifications.

"Fuck technology," Kat replied, "I'll decline all I can. I heard about a girl from New Birmingham who died a week after having a well-monitored pregnancy."

Lucy held her hand to her face and shook her head. "That's awful, but it wouldn't have anything to do with the modifications."

Kat's wavy locks swished across her face as she shook her

head. "Fuck Technology!"

"That's what Mia's doing, fucking technology." Ellie stroked her bump and grinned at Mia. "I bet you don't have any baby plans."

Mia wanted to scratch her eyes out, she wanted a baby more than anything, but she stayed calm. Her confidence from being with Tyler had given her more composure. "Tyler's asked if we could have a Tushi-Baby. I've not decided yet."

Kat raised an eyebrow and rested her chin on her hand.

"It would be weird," Lucy said.

Tushi Babies were not uncommon but were there to appease Tushi Wives. Men choosing Tushi-Wives instead of their human counterparts had become popular. A beautiful woman with a perfect figure, content to do all the chores whilst the guy played or watched esports. The guys, like Mia, had amazing sex whenever they desired and granted their Tushi wives, the small request for a baby.

"If I go along with it, I'll have a mini-bump attached, which tracks my personality to shape the fresh mind." Mia quite liked the idea but was nervous. If she agreed, she'd be the first woman to have a Tushi baby.

"Developing an early bond by talking to your future offspring, clever stuff," Lucy said.

Ellie suggested, "you may as well join the baby club, even if it's a Tushi baby. What else are you going to do other than run your little coffee shop with your mom?"

"I run it on my own!" Mia resisted a full-on attack for the hormonal Ellie. "My mom gave me the business as a parting gift when she moved in with her new fella. I enjoy running it and chatting to my regulars." Mia sighed, "It's fine for now, but someday I'd like to be famous for more than just making cakes in a little shop."

"Being the first woman to have a Tushi Baby would make you famous," Kat said.

"I'd rather be designing or controlling them, like Ethan."

"Somebody's still in love with their Ex," Kat gave her a cheesy grin. "He'll be at the wedding. Perhaps you could design a robot together."

"Don't think so, I've moved on. I'll stick with Tyler." She jumped up and gave a quick twirl. "We've been practicing a dance."

"Go, girl! You've come out of your shell since we were kids," Lucy said.

Mia smiled. "Thanks to Tyler."

"You don't want Ethan back then," Kat asked.

"I'm with Tyler now. Ethan couldn't say or do anything to change that!" Mia took a large swig of her wine hoping the subject would move on.

Kat received notification. "Our Chinese delights are here." She headed to the door and Mia followed.

The drone was a sturdy unit, with four one metre fans holding the mini-bot steady as it came to rest before being released. The mini bot wheeled up to and through the door as Kat welcomed it in. It stopped next to the table and opened to release its steam filled payload. Kat unloaded the contents as mouths watered. The mini bot rolled away and Mia watched as it slotted back into its drone and lifted above the buildings to speed away.

Despite drone delivered food being the norm for many, Kat often cooked for Mirek, but tonight was a treat whilst she relaxed with her friends. The food hit the spot as they continued to chat, reminiscing about how they'd played up their parents. The spiciest stories as always came from Kat who when prompted by Ellie, re-told the familiar tale of when outside the restroom in a restaurant, she showed a young lad her breasts. Her Mom grounded her when she overheard the boy returning to his seat saying some crazy girl had asked him to feel her tits. Kat cowering in her seat had given her away.

An innocent comment from Lucy changed the tone. "How long have you been with Mirek?"

"She moved in here the same night they met. They were engaged within the week," Mia blurted out.

Kat bobbed her tongue out at Mia and replied, "Four Months. When you know, you know."

"Four months! Are you crazy?" Lucy said. A blush returned to Kat's cheeks as Mia and Ellie sniggered.

Kat composed herself. "Yep, crazy in love." She stared at the video wall for a moment and stroked her chin. All eyes were fixed on Kat as she contemplated.

"I don't know when his birthday is, or if he likes Christmas. I don't *really* know if he's happy I'm having his baby." Kat turned to Mia, "What am I doing? Have I gone crazy?"

As maid of honor, it was Mia's job to re-assure her, "Yes, you're crazy, you always have been. Mirek is impetuous too. If you love him, marry him, you'll find out lots more about him, some you'll like, some you won't, but if you love him, you'll get through them."

"I bet you haven't even farted in front of each other yet," Ellie said.

Kat didn't reply, but her silence confirmed they both had a lot to learn about each other. Her confidence returned with a strong smile. "I love Mirek. I never want to let him go and I'm marrying him tomorrow, even if his farts stink." They giggled and joked about stinky boys. "It's why we wear perfume," Kat said.

Kat had planned the night to perfection. They changed into their PJ's and settled down for their sleepover. She put on her favorite old movie and insisted they sang along to, 'The Rocky Horror Picture Show,' and insisted they got on their feet to do the time warp.

A hard knock on the door stopped the dancing. A sense of foreboding washed over them all, apart from the scheming Ellie, who paused the film. With a dressing gown protecting her modesty, she strolled over to the door. Kat called out, "If it's Mirek tell him he can't come in. He can't see me until tomorrow."

Ellie opened the door a fraction and there were some mumbling voices before she welcomed in a hunky policeman. He stood with his fists on his hips, "Kat Parker, you are under arrest and need to join us at the station."

"Get lost. I'm getting married tomorrow," Kat said.

"You are under arrest for public indecency in a restaurant."

"What! From ten years ago?" She glared at Ellie, who was already sniggering.

"You can take your punishment here." The handsome policeman smiled bringing fun to the occasion.

He pulled up a chair. "Would you like to take a seat?"

"No thanks." Kat folded her arms.

The policeman grabbed her arm and pulled her into the seat. He stood directly in front of her and removed his jacket to reveal his pumped body of bulging muscles.

Kat looked over to Ellie and gave her a wry smile.

The fake policeman placed his hand on her chin and guided her attention back to him, "Undo my belt and pants."

In the spirit of the fun, Kat obliged, until the size of the bulge in his boxers became clear. This was no ordinary stripper gram, he was a sexbot. He then pulled out his sizeable shaft. "Milk me," he ordered.

"No thanks Mate, too much for me." She pushed back against his sixpack and raised from the chair.

With Kat's mind made up, Ellie said, "Okay, never mind. The show's over. Let's get back to the film."

They expected him to leave, but he returned to the same stance with his fists on his waist, "My mission is not complete. If not Kat, who?"

Ellie shrugged at the critical stares from Kat, Mia and Lucy, before she stepped towards the menacing figure, "Okay! What's your mission?"

"I need to be unloaded before I can return to my station."

Ellie shook her head. "No thanks. We've paid. You can go." Ellie waved towards the door and returned to her seat.

He was unmoved. The girls ignored him and returned to the film, but every couple of minutes he repeated his task getting louder each time. "Unload me!"

"I'll call to complain," Ellie said, but the droid took the mobile and tossed it onto the lounger and took Kat by the arm.

Mia screamed at him and grabbed his arm. "She's fucking pregnant, leave her alone."

Lucy grabbed another arm. "We want you to leave!"

Ellie retrieved her mobile and punched and swiped at the screen.

The droid overpowered Kat, Mia and Lucy, as he pulled them towards the bedroom. As they reached the bedroom door, he removed his grip on Kat.

"Send your feedback, or I'll be back."

He straightened his pants and picked up his jacket as he left.

Sighs were let out as Ellie closed the door. "I tried to cancel the booking, but it didn't work. Instead, I confirmed the task was complete and thankfully it worked."

Kat placed a reassuring hand on Ellie's shoulder. "Sorry to wimp out." Intent on lifting the mood, she continued, "It may have been better to have done the deed rather than have all the screaming. Mia, you squeal like a pig."

Laughter followed before Ellie restarted the film and they settled back into their loungers.

Mia didn't join in the giggles. When she spoke, the laughter stopped, "Why didn't he stop when you asked?"

"I guess he wanted to complete his job." Ellie shrugged

"They're programmed to listen and respond, not carry on regardless."

"Mia, stop flapping, everything's okay," Kat added.

"You can't ignore what happened. That was wrong."

"She's worried Tyler might start ordering her about," Ellie said.

"The drama's over. Watch the film," Kat said.

When the credits rolled for the end of their emotion filled night, they were ready for sleep. Apart from Mia. Her mind whirred all night. She wanted to have a family, but would a droid family give her the life she wanted. Tyler was her lover and protector, but what would she do if he went rogue like the stripper droid?

Awoken is available on Amazon Kindle unlimited, eBook and paperback)

26yr old Mia hoped for a peaceful life when she chose to be with Tyler, a fully functioning AI droid, but a past love aims to bring her down from the clouds.

With the wedding of Kat and Mirek approaching the trepidation of seeing her previous boyfriend Ethan has lifted. A more confident Mia is more than ready for anything Ethan (her Ex) could say. Having the impeccable Tyler on her arm had made her bullet proof but a handwritten note from Ethan (her Ex) breaks through her perfect world and tests her resolve for the love of her life.

Lucy's love life finally gains some traction, but when she finds out about Femalatism, Mia and Ethan are called to help.

Ethan reveals a change in the network which will change the way droids are perceived but when he is frozen out by the Tushi Corporation what can he do?